For the mystery lover...

DEATH ON FRATERNITY ROW

A PREQUEL

THE KAITLYNN DAHL MYSTERIES
BOOK ZERO

K.D. UPTON

CHAPTER 1

*T*he coffin clapped shut in front of a makeshift altar.

"One more time." I snapped consecutive pictures, each with a different pose. "That'll do it."

Flickering candles on whitewashed pillars surrounded the casket, lending a yellowish glow. Scattered among them were pumpkins, along with orange, yellow, and white mums. The biggest eye-catcher was a twenty-four-by-thirty inch portrait of a young man hung from the wall behind it all. Black silk covered the three bay windows lining the left wall, and the antique oak coffee table, burgundy chaise lounge chairs, and the two black leather couches had been pushed against the opposite wall, opening the expansive room for the rows of folding chairs, each adorned with a single red rose.

A blonde goddess of a woman with saucer-shaped green eyes bounced over as I reviewed the pictures on the camera.

"Should we be doing this?" Her pert nose scrunched up in distaste. "It feels… sacrilegious."

I scrolled through the series of photos, pausing over one in particular. The woman beamed from behind the food table, which was conveniently centered between the candlelit pillars but in front of the coffin. On the food table sat a black and white skeleton cake. Long blonde hair fell forward against the woman's shoulders as she held up a gleaming knife in her right hand, exposing an expensive gold bracelet and a bold dragon tattoo with a blue tail on her inner wrist. Her impish smile lit up her face. Krissy Fox, Connor Byrne's girlfriend, and ruler of all Alpha Pi's girlfriends. She was queen bee when it came to do's and don'ts for the female partners of the fraternity brothers. Although she was tough nosed, I liked her.

"It's my job." I glanced up at my dearest friend and grinned. "Halloween parties are supposed to be fun, remember? Fun? It's what we're supposed to be doing in our college years."

Skylar Wren bunched up her nose again. "You're pre-med, Kaitlynn. I get it, but skeletons freak me out." She shivered. "They're meant to be buried, not an attraction for frat boys having a binger." Her blonde hair bobbed around her shoulders as she shook her head.

"It's not like it's real. Ashton bought it from a party store. Relax." I patted her on the shoulder and held up the camera. "Look. Krissy's having a great time."

Skylar peered at the camera, looking skeptical. "Are you sure he got it from a party store? There's something off about it."

I noted her narrowed eyes and pursed lips. She was staring hard at the coffin like at any minute the skeleton would leap up and walk out of the room.

"Are you okay, Sky?"

She nodded, a smile lighting up her beautiful face. "Yep. What's next?"

While she tried to seem alright, her eyes spoke otherwise, but I'd learned long ago not to push. When Skylar was ready to talk, she'd let me know.

"Uh, let's see." I let the camera drape against my chest and pulled out the slip of paper in my back pocket. "Black and orange streamers." I scratched my head and searched the room. "Where could they be?" I mumbled and walked out of the ballroom and down the stairs before realizing Skylar wasn't behind me. When I looked back, she was still standing in front of the pillars eyeing the skeleton in the coffin.

I strode through the foyer, veering left, past an old-fashioned photo booth, a candy dispensing machine full of bubblegum and red licorice, and a bulletin board with this week's cleaning schedule. Looked like Ashton was on toilets this week. I bet he'd already paid someone to do it for him like all his other fraternity brothers. These guys came from wealth, and I stifled a grin at the thought of any of them lifting a finger to dust, let alone scrub a commode.

Stepping into the restaurant-sized kitchen, I scanned the room, zeroing in on my boyfriend of a year. Well, almost a year. It was more like eleven months, ten days, and two hours since we'd made it official.

"Hey." I walked up, unsure. As I passed the commercial ovens, a mousy brunette appeared in front of Ashton. She dropped a hand from his bicep, stuffing it into the pocket of her skinny jeans.

"Hi, Katie," she said, her lips twitching at the corners. "I was just asking Ash if he needed anything for the party."

I stared at Ashton, but he'd taken an interest in a spot on the stainless steel countertops, rubbing his finger over something multiple times until I cleared my throat.

"Yeah... I bet. So, Ashton..." he caught my gaze, "where are the black and orange streamers? I've looked in the ballroom, but—"

"Right." He jumped into action, striding toward me without so much as a glance at Victoria. Cupping my elbow, he led me out of the kitchen and into the foyer, where I jerked free.

"Why is she here, Ash? What were you doing in there?"

Ashton shifted his weight nervously. Luckily we were alone. "Nothing." He lowered his voice, pleading. "Come on, babe. You're my girl." He glanced at the stairwell leading to the ballroom every few seconds.

I crossed my arms against my chest. "Why is she here?"

Ashton shrugged. "Jamie and Vic are on again. Can we go find the streamers now?"

"Jamie? He's bringing Amber. Try again."

Ashton's jaw twitched. "I don't keep track of their love lives, alright?" He stormed toward the stairs and climbed them two at a time, disappearing into the ballroom.

I took a cleansing breath and slowly climbed the stairs. I entered the ballroom to a flurry of activity. With their dates ogling from the sidelines, loads of frat guys set up round tables and chairs while yet another set up his disc jockey equipment. He bobbed his head to the beat of a popular pop song blaring from the overhead speakers.

Ashton waved from close to the casket. I marched over, smiling at the chef currently flipping a sizzling steak, its juices dropping onto the hot grill while I willed my grumbling stomach to cease complaining. The last thing I'd eaten, scratch that, the only thing I'd eaten today was a banana and black coffee. I glanced at my watch; it was already half past five. That banana was twelve hours ago.

Ashton picked up a cardboard box and tipped it over, shaking it before tossing it to the ground. "They were in here this morning."

I barely heard him over the blasting music. "I can go get some."

Ashton shook his head. "It's my responsibility, babe. Let me." But his sights weren't on me anymore.

I craned my neck toward the direction he was looking and noticed none other than Vic. She was unabashedly staring at us, tight jeans and all. If they were any tighter, they'd have to cut her out of them.

Digging my nails into my palms, I forced a grin. "It's alright. I forgot my dress this morning in the rush to get here."

"Are you sure?" Ashton clasped my shoulders, his face inches from mine. "You're a lifesaver, babe." He abruptly let go and stalked off toward the door, and Vic.

An arm draped across my shoulder. "He's a jerkwad, Kaitlynn. You can do so much better." She hooked a thumb toward the door. "Olivia's on her way. Let's forget about the guys for a night, alright? Come on. Those streamers aren't buying themselves."

I offered a grateful smile and we strolled arm-in-arm through the ballroom, stopping short a few feet later. Raised voices drew everyone's attention to the DJ's table.

"What's your problem?" Trent Dixon, a rugby player and all around jerk, barked. He slammed a can of beer and crunched it against his chest, belching into the face of Bradley Roberts. "You're squashing the buzz."

4

Bradley stood, fists balled at his sides, seething in anger. Face bright red, he was rooted to the spot.

Trent slapped a picture onto Bradley's chest. "There's more where that came from, pal." He shoved Bradley into the DJ table, knocking it over and sending the electronics crashing to the floor.

"Hey!" The DJ jumped sideways, watching his expensive equipment go flying. "You're paying if anything's broken, Trent!"

Trent was already down the stairs and out of sight. Bradley shoved the picture into his pant pocket and bent to pick up the music equipment. The chatter soon resumed, and thankfully so did the music. Rap this time.

Skylar and I descended the stairs. "What was that all about?" She whispered.

I shrugged. "Who knows? Trent's always causing trouble."

"Yeah, someone ought to put him in his place. One day it'll happen. I just hope we're around to see it." She squeezed my shoulder, stopping me directly in front of the front door. "Tonight, though, is all about fun, right? What's better than dressing up, eating good food, on the men, and making you the belle of the night. I've got a surprise, and before you protest, hear me out. Olivia's bringing her makeup bag. Tonight's all about the ladies!" She squealed with glee, and as if on cue, the front door opened, Olivia's head popped in.

"Who's ready to play?" She shook a travel-on sized suitcase bag that sounded like there were fifty rocks inside. "He won't be able to take his eyes off you, lady."

They both whisked me out the door, but when I looked back into the home, my heart sank. Not only was Victoria dressed in a plunging, sparkling sequence gown that made her eyes pop and her skin look radiant, but Ashton was by her side, their arms linked. She lifted on her tippy toes and kissed his cheek.

"That will take a miracle," I mumbled.

CHAPTER 2

*J*t only took five minutes to purchase the streamers, and then we headed to my apartment. I'd hung my gown from the bathroom door the night before to avoid wrinkles. I stood back and admired the floor length powder blue chiffon dress, and my friends admired it with me. It had taken ages to find it. Olivia, Skylar, and I had taken an afternoon last weekend and shopped around, but with my measly budget, we'd ended up at the co-op store. I'm not complaining. Lots of beautiful pieces were donated weekly, some with their tags still attached. Once, Skylar had found a Gucci dress and splurged. We teased her for months about it because she'd worn it to bed that night. From that point on, we'd made weekly visits, mostly for fun. None of us was rich.

"It's gorgeous!" Skylar gushed, rubbing the chiffon between her fingers. "Look at the details. With your rack, Ashton won't notice anything else."

I playfully slapped her hand, and she dropped the gown. She perched next to Olivia on the bed, watching with amusement as she crammed a cheeseburger into her petite mouth. Olivia had threatened us within an inch of our lives if we hadn't stopped off at the local burger joint, and now the greasy smell of fries and burgers hung in the air.

"Shev'es rought," Olivia garbled, her mouth full of burger. She swallowed and sucked down some of her soda. "It's beautiful, Kaitlynn. He's a right arse if he takes up with Victoria Bedingford." She grimaced. "What a louse."

Skylar smirked. "You mean a witch with a capital B."

Olivia arched a brow. "If the shoe fits..."

I slid a finger over the tight bodice of my gown and smiled. They were right. I'd struck gold with this one. Zipping up the dress bag, I carefully draped it over my arm, picking up the streamer bag with the other.

"Alright, ladies. Are we ready?"

Olivia wiped a napkin over her ketchup stained lips and picked up my purse from the bed. "One thing... are the guys you set us up with pushy?"

Skylar gazed off into the distance next to her. She often appeared miles away. We chalked it up to her being flighty, but I'd always wondered if it was something else.

"Uh, yeah. They're perfect gentlemen. Ashton promises they'll behave."

Olivia rolled her eyes. "That's a relief," she grumbled. "If Master Ashton, lord of the manor, says they're gentlemen, then who are we to disagree? Am I right, Sky?"

Olivia peered at Skylar, still miles away. "Hey..." She nudged Sky's arm.

Skylar blinked. "What?" It was as if she had snapped out of a trance. "Oh yes. They're complete gentlemen. I've seen them around campus, and they never litter."

"Oh my" Olivia splayed her hand on her chest, batting her lashes. "An environmentalist. I'm swooning already."

"Mock if you will, but the Earth matters, and I, for one, appreciate a man who cares."

Olivia snorted. "That and six-pack abs."

Skylar frowned. "It's not all about the physique."

7

"Isn't it?" Olivia charged. "Name one guy you dated that didn't fit the jock stereotype. Go ahead. We'll wait."

Skylar opened and closed her mouth multiple times before standing and heading for the bedroom door. "Tonight starts a new trend."

Both Olivia and I squashed a giggle and followed her out.

* * *

WHEN WE ARRIVED BACK at the Alpha Pi fraternity house, the outside slate walkway was lit up with tiny pumpkin lights strewn with fake cobwebs. The pale brick exterior glowed orange and purple under a flashing strobe light someone had planted in the yard. It was an enormous home with one residential wing resembling dorm rooms, albeit a rich man's idea of them. The other wing held the ballroom up the stairwell to the left of the front door. Behind that, and off to the left, was a meeting room of sorts. Leather couches and tables were strewn throughout, mostly for studying or fraternity meetings. There was an opening into the kitchen, so the men ate in this room as well. They also held party nights here, reserving the ballroom only for formal events and initiations.

Olivia, Skylar, and I strolled up, arms full of party gowns, streamers, and makeup bags. I jutted my hip and hit the doorbell. The door creaked open, and we stepped inside the darkened foyer. "The Monster Mash" played over the speakers, and a court jester popped out from the residential wing to our right.

"Greetings, fair maidens, and welcome to Alpha Pi's Halloween Bash." He bowed, jingling the bells on his jester's hat. Standing upright, he grinned, shoving his hat about his ears. "If you wish to freshen up, please use the designated restroom in the fraternity meeting hall. Are any of you interested in a beverage? Perhaps a witch's brew? A vampire's kiss? Or what about a corpse reviver?"

He held out a silver platter with multiple drinks brimming with smoke drifting out of them.

"Ah, no thanks, Connor. Maybe later." I readjusted the bundle in my arms and stepped toward the common room, blocked off as the ladies' dressing room and bathroom for tonight's event.

Connor backstepped out of the room only to step in once again when the next set of girlfriends appeared at the door. He was an amiable guy, always minding his business and never passing up the chance to play Dungeons and Dragons, thus the jester's outfit. It was the rage at the frat house, and the girlfriends always knew that Thursday nights were off limits because of it. None of us heard a peep out of them. Not even a text. I wasn't familiar with the game, but they sure loved it. Next to the game, Connor was most devoted to his girlfriend. That was the thing I admired the most about him; his devotion to Krissy. He doted on her, granting every whim, from grabbing cappuccinos on the fly to buying her tampons if it was her time of the month. He was the best boyfriend, and a part of me craved that.

My friends and I ambled into the dressing room and dumped our belongings onto the couches. I arched my aching back, twisting to get the kinks out. It was time I started running again. This freshman fifteen was becoming twenty.

Skylar secured the door and pulled off her ripped sweatshirt and leggings. "When do we meet our dates?" she asked. She stepped one foot, then the other, into a slinky fuchsia gown that glided over her like water. It was a simple silk slip dress, but somehow, anything Skylar wore looked good enough for the runway. Most people always asked why I hung around her because guys would never notice me in her presence, but I didn't care. Sky and I preferred our own type of guy. She loved the jocks, and I loved nerds. Though Ashton was different. He'd stormed in like a hurricane and swept me off my feet the second I entered freshman comp.

"As soon as we get done here. I've texted them to give us another fifteen minutes. Ashton says they're eager to meet you."

Olivia hovered her lipstick over her plump lips. "Eager? Are they socially inept? Please tell me you haven't set us up with guys only a mother would love."

"Give me some credit." I stepped into my gown, motioning for Sky to zip me up. Spinning around, I looked expectantly at my friends. "Well? What do you think?"

Both of them grinned.

Skylar winked. "You look fabulous, Kaitlynn."

"I agree. At least your dress fits." Olivia tugged at her gown, her bosoms on full view. "I'm practically giving a peep show in this number."

I giggled. "The dress is stunning, as are you, my friend. Have you never worn a plunging neckline before?"

Olivia nibbled on her lower lip. "My parents forbade it. They're rather conservative."

I took her hands in mine and drew her to the full-length mirror the men had set up for us, which was thoughtful.

"Look at you. It won't be me stopping the show, Olivia. It's you."

She was stunning. Even Skylar nodded approvingly.

"I don't know." Olivia cocked her head, staring at her reflection in the mirror. Unease marked her face. "Are you sure?"

Skylar rested her chin on Olivia's shoulder from behind and looked into the mirror. "One hundred percent. Plus, it's too late. The dress shops are closed."

Olivia sighed. "Fine, but this guy better be worth it."

We got ready within another thirty minutes, and it was a good thing because the room had filled up fast.

Stopping by the door, I placed my hand on the knob and turned to face my friends. "Ready?"

Olivia smoothed down the front of her full skirt while Skylar squared her shoulders. Her blonde hair hung in waves about her shoulders. "Ready," they said in unison.

We stepped out into the darkness of the foyer and walked until we made it by the ballroom stairs. I squinted into the dark lit with only candles and spotted the two dates for my friends.

"Here we go." I gripped a hand of each and stepped forward. "Marcus and Ben, meet your dates, Olivia and Skylar."

Olivia held out a shaky hand toward Marcus. "Um, nice to meet you, Marcus."

He shook her hand warmly and held up a wrist corsage. "I hope you like lilies."

Olivia gaped at the beautiful corsage. "They're my favorite."

He placed the corsage on and they walked arm in arm to the ballroom. Olivia turned around and mouthed, "He's hot" to me.

Skylar took the initiative and thrust out her hand. "Ben, there are rules. No kissing, no fanny patting, no boob grazing, got it?"

Ben's eyebrows shot upward. "Uh… yeah, that's fine." He stuck out his elbow. "I'm sorry, but I didn't realize we needed corsages."

Skylar looked down at his elbow and then looped hers through his. "Fields are where flowers belong."

Ben smiled broadly. "I agree." He stood up, nerves forgotten. "What's your major?"

I watched them walk across the foyer and up the stairs to the ballroom, feeling proud of myself. While Ben wasn't the typical man Skylar dated, he was attractive, fit, and smart. He'd be a match for her feisty yet flighty temperament. As for Olivia, how could I not set her up with the hottest guy? Next to Ashton, of course. She rarely saw the beauty the rest of us did, too engrossed in her studies to look up from a book. Men admired her even when she wore sweats and a ponytail. Skylar was gorgeous, but Olivia was radiant. It was sad that she couldn't see it.

"Vic, for the last time—"

I spun upon hearing Ashton's disgruntled voice. My smile all but faded when I realized Victoria was holding his hand.

I turned and stormed off.

"Kaitlynn, wait!"

CHAPTER 3

$\mathcal{A}$shton released her hand and hurried after me, but I was hoping to be anywhere other than there. Up the ballroom stairs I flew, my footsteps pounding all the way, into the roaring party. The scent of alcohol hit my nose as I weaved through the dancing, jumping, swaying crowd. After getting jostled a few times, I finally saw my friends at the DJ table and made my way over.

"Kaitlynn..."

A firm grip on my arm halted me in my tracks. A young woman dressed in an ivory laced, beaded maxi dress more fitting for a wedding than a formal, spun at both of us as we stood between her and her date.

"Watch it," she said, along with a few terse words which do not bear repeating. She'd clearly drunk a few too many spirits already.

Tears brimmed my eyelashes, and I fought to blink them back. "It's fine, Ash." The effort to speak stung my throat.

In an attempt to appear calm, Ashton leaned in, his jaw tight. An overwhelming sense of panic radiated from him.

"It's not what it looked like, Kaitlynn. Vic wants Jamie back. That's all."

"She has to hold your hand to do it?"

I diverted my gaze towards the group of dancers. A slow song played, and the ladies leaned their heads against their dates' shoulders, completely engrossed in the moment.

"Kaitlynn," he took my hand, tilting my head up with a finger under my chin. He observed the shimmering sequins on the strapless gown, paying special attention to the full bodice. This was his first time seeing me in formal attire. After a moment, he shook his head, a smile growing over his handsome face. "You look marvelous."

He drew me close, encircling my waist with his arms. Pressing his lips to my temple, he murmured, "You're the only one."

With closed eyes, I let the music carry me away, tuning out the crowd and the past, and leaned into him, catching a whiff of his musky cologne mixed with a hint of soap.

After a few moments, the music picked up, and I withdrew slightly, lowering my gaze to our intertwined hands. His long, lean fingers were those of an accountant or financier. They'd never seen a hard day's work while mine toiled in the garden, at a restaurant, or any other job fit for working. Though I was a pharmacist's daughter, our lineage was of Vikings and Scots, used to laboring. From my pale hand to his tanned one, we were opposites. I was studying pre-med, all thanks to my demanding mother, and he was studying business like his father and grandfather before him. Born to generational wealth, they were charming and polite, but after our first meeting, I got the keen impression that they only tolerated me. I was a fling, something to get out of his system. Prestigious families only wed into prestigious families, and while mine were both pharmacists, it wasn't enough. We were new money, and there wasn't anything worse than new money.

In an instant, Ashton's adoring face became filled with rage. He went from gazing into my eyes to shoving me aside in a matter of seconds.

Something slammed into my back, knocking the breath right out of me. The room spun and I careened sideways. Ashton lunged for me but it was too late. With a grunt, I crashed onto the wooden floor, hitting my head.

"Whoa!" Ashton knelt beside me, a hand held up in warning. The music shut off. "Take it outside, Trent. Not in here." To me, he said, "Are you okay? Can you sit?"

"Kaitlynn?" I heard Skylar's high-pitched squeal. She was by my side in no time. After hiking up her slender skirt, she sank to the floor on her knees. "What happened?"

"Trent pissing people off again. One day he'll meet a bigger bully." Ashton frowned. "Do you need ice?" He beckoned over a frat brother with a snap of his fingers, ordering him to grab a plastic bag of ice and a towel. The frat brother rushed off before I could say otherwise.

"It's only a bump." I propped up on my elbow, immediately regretting it. My stomach churned with the movement.

"She's green." Olivia had arrived, Marcus in tow. "How many fingers am I holding up?"

I breathed in. "Three. I'm fine. It's just that I haven't eaten since this morning."

Ashton ordered the chef to bring over a slice of bread with butter, and I nibbled on it, growing redder by the second. The party had come to a halt, and I despised being the focal point. That was Skylar's role, and while I'd like to think they were all staring at her, I knew better.

As if sensing my tension, Skylar called out to the DJ, "Play something. Anything."

Thankfully, the music started up again, a little softer this time.

"Here. Let me help you up." Ashton offered a hand and pulled me up.

With shaky legs, I pressed the back of my hand to my sweaty forehead. No telling what my makeup looked like. "I need to freshen up. Sky and Olivia, would you help me, please?"

Legs threatening to give way, I clung to my friends, allowing them to lead me out of the ballroom. Right after we landed in the foyer, I saw a woman engaged in a heated argument with the jester near the residential entrance wing. Her arms flailed wildly as she spoke with great intensity.

"You cretin!" The young blonde shoved a colorful scarf into Connor's shocked face.

His expression shifted from confusion to alarm. Usually calm, his jaw was clenched, his eyes darting around the room with a mix of disbelief and anger. "Krissy, it's just a scarf."

Krissy's usually cheerful face was contorted with frustration, her brows furrowed and lips pursed.

The air in the room became heavy. The once harmonious facade of the couple had shattered, replaced by a raw sense of frustration and betrayal.

Their voices echoed through the fraternity house, drawing fellow frat brothers to peek out of the ballroom with curious expressions.

It was like peering behind a curtain, revealing the imperfections that lay beneath. Krissy and Connor, the epitome of a picture-perfect couple, had been exposed as the flawed human beings they were.

They remained silent, their faces red and their breathing labored.

"*Just* a scarf?" Krissy jammed her hands on her curvy hips.

"I accidentally picked it up with my books. It's a mistake." Connor yanked off his jester's hat.

Krissy puffed out her reddened cheeks and stepped backward. With a shake of her head, she outstretched her hand, blocking him from getting closer. "You bet it's a mistake. All the years I spent with you? I gave you..." She held her hand to her mouth, struggling to rein in her emotions. "Everything," she whispered.

Krissy spun and stalked off toward the ladies' restroom, Connor hot on her heels, his bells jangling with each step.

"Krissy! Krissy, wait!"

"Smooth, brother. Real smooth."

A man with sandy-brown hair appeared from the shadows near the chore board, swaying slightly. Amidst the stench of alcohol and urine, he raised a beer can to his mouth and took a sip.

"Not now, Trent," Connor barked, pushing past him.

Trent paid him no mind. "Why bother with a sedan when you can ride a Mercedes, right?"

Krissy jolted to a stop directly in front of Trent's swaying form.

15

She reared her hand back and slapped Trent so hard his head snapped sideways.

Skylar, Olivia, and I stared on, unable to speak.

Trent rubbed his red jaw and smirked, watching Krissy run off into the ladies' room and slam the door shut behind her. He tipped his head towards us and strolled off into the kitchen, probably in search of another stash of beer.

"Uh, should we go in there?" Olivia asked, looking from me to Sky.

Skylar didn't have time to answer because Connor jogged up.

"Hey, could you do me a solid and check on Krissy?" he asked. "She's got this all wrong."

"We're on it," I said without thinking. Skylar gave me a look that meant I'd lost my ever-loving mind. "Is there anything you want us to tell her?"

Connor stuffed his hands in his pockets, his head bowed like a kid who'd been caught with a hand in the cookie jar. "Only that I love her."

"We'll see what we can do, Connor. Go back into the party."

Color flooded his pale cheeks. "Thanks, Kaitlynn." He gripped my hand. "I owe you one."

He jogged up the steps and disappeared into the ballroom with the other fraternity brothers patting his back.

I stared at both my friends, who each held questioning expressions. Those looks said it all. How would I ever rectify this? Should I? Yet there was no time to think or even back out of it. I'd committed to the task. With a renewed sense of purpose, I set off for the ladies' room, Olivia and Skylar a step behind.

By the time we entered the women's restroom, Krissy had used up half a box of tissues. Her trembling hands struggled to tear another tissue from the box as she wiped at the streaks of black mascara running down her cheeks. She had puffy, swollen eyes from crying, and her usual sparkle was gone.

I gently reached out and placed a hand on her stooped shoulder. Strands of hair stuck to the sides of her face. I handed her a new tissue, which she gratefully took, dabbing at her eyes and trying to compose herself. Eventually, her trembling subsided.

We stood in silence for a moment, the distant sounds of laughter from the ballroom above seeping into the restroom.

Krissy looked toward the ceiling and closed her puffy eyes. "He said he loved me. I... I... can't believe he'd do this to me." She sucked in two breaths. "To us." She blew into a tissue and tossed it into the trash bin next to the full-length mirror.

I led her to the couch, noting a tray of cheeses and sausages on a nearby table. After clearing a place for her to sit, I snagged a tray of food and brought it over, offering her some, but she waved it off. I took a couple of crackers and sausage and handed the tray to Sky, stuffing a mini sausage in my mouth before turning back to Krissy. I'd need all my strength for this conversation.

I crouched down in front of her, placing my hand on her knee to offer a small measure of comfort. "Listen, I'm sure there's a simple explanation. Maybe it was an accident after all."

Krissy dropped her head into her hands and sobbed. Shoulders bobbing, she choked out, "He's... he's... been lying to me. I've sm- smelled perfume on h-him. *Perfume!*"

Okay, so that was harder to dismiss.

"What was his explanation when you confronted him?"

Krissy stared down at her hands and pulled a tissue apart, laying each strand in a pile on her satin gown. "I didn't."

I brushed the wet strands of hair off her cheeks. "Why not?"

Krissy licked her lips and shrugged. "I don't know if I could handle it."

One glance at my friends, and I knew immediately they understood. We stood together and enveloped Krissy in a warm hug. Her shoulders trembled beneath us, but we held on until the worst had passed. When we moved aside, she was genuinely smiling.

"Why are you being so nice to me?"

"Why shouldn't we be? Listen, on the surface, I won't lie, it looks bad. But that doesn't mean Connor has cheated. If he has, isn't that something you need to find out?"

Krissy's eyelashes glittered with a fresh round of tears. "What if I lose him? If he cheated, why wasn't I good enough for him? Is there something wrong with me?"

I waited for her to catch her breath. "You are good enough. It wasn't anything you did or didn't do. If he's cheated, then that's on him, Krissy, not you. You've got your whole life ahead. Don't waste it on some guy in college if he can't see what a treasure you are."

Behind me, Skylar snorted, mumbling, "Good advice. Maybe you should practice what you preach."

I shot her a brief glare, redirecting my attention to Krissy.

"It's only ever been Connor," Krissy said, her voice soft and fragile. She dabbed at her wet cheeks with a new tissue.

"Yeah, that's tough. You've been dating for how long?"

"Four years." She sniffled. "He proposed to me last spring."

Wow. That *was* serious.

I clasped her hand in mine. "Hey, he wanted me to tell you something."

Krissy boldly stared at me, shaking her head. "I can't. I can't bear the lies anymore."

I glanced at Sky, who looked just as confused as me, and Olivia wasn't any better.

"Alright, but hear him out first. After you talk if you don't like what he's said, then end it."

Krissy tugged at the tissue in her lap.

"He told me he loves you. If you're engaged, don't you owe it to yourself to have one last conversation?"

Krissy sighed heavily. "Fine, but I'm getting an Uber just in case."

She pulled out her cell and then gathered herself. She walked out of the dressing room five minutes later, leaving us on the couches tired, weary, and hungry.

"Gosh, I didn't know they were engaged." Olivia draped one leg over the couch arm, gnawing on a mini sausage.

"Who could he have cheated with?" Skylar asked, snacking on some cheese on the opposite couch. "Didn't you say they were the 'it' couple?"

It was as much of a shock to me as my friends, probably because I knew them so well. Since dating Ashton, we'd been inseparable from the frat and their girlfriends. It was a sort of tribe, and every Saturday night meant another frat party, and Connor and Krissy were the belles of the ball each time. Everyone secretly compared themselves to them, but in reality, it had been a facade. How sad.

"Yeah, but doesn't everyone have secrets?" I chomped on my third cheese and sausage cracker, feeling my tongue stick to the roof of my mouth and the cracker slide down my throat in a gob. It was time for a drink.

"Speaking of secrets," Skylar leaned forward, her sharp green eyes keen on me, "what's going on between Ashton and Victoria? She's been undressing him with her eyes all night. Who's she here with, anyway?"

Who *was* she here with? If she and Jamie were really trying to work it out, then why did he bring Amber? And since he brought Amber, how did Victoria get in? Formals included the fraternity brothers and dates only. If she wasn't with Jamie, then who? I sat up.

"What?" Skylar asked, interest flashed across her face.

"It's time for a little reconnaissance." I eyed both my friends, who were dusting cracker crumbs from their lips. "Who's up for finding out about Victoria?"

Skylar's eyes sparkled with mischief. "If we're doing this, then Ashton's not off limits. Agreed?"

Skylar was pushing me like normal, but this meant I couldn't bury my head in the sand anymore. If Ashton and Victoria were dating behind my back, I'd finally find out, and I'd have to confront it once and for all.

I held my chin high. "Agreed."

"Then what are we waiting for?" Skylar clapped her hands together, grinning. "Let the games begin."

CHAPTER 4

*H*and in hand, Skylar and I walked to the restroom door, swinging our hands back and forth.

"Hey, Ashton isn't my favorite pers—"

"You hate him, Skylar."

"Hate's a strong word. Let's go with a strong dislike. Anyway, a little birdie told me Ash didn't cheat on you."

I came to a halt, fixated on her. My heart raced so rapidly it felt as though it would burst. "But he was holding her hand and—"

"Nope," Olivia chimed in, opening the door. "He was leading her out of the house. Marcus said Ash wanted her gone. She was causing a problem for Jamie. Whatever you saw was taken out of context. The dude's an honest Abe."

I smirked. "Dude? Honest Abe? What's gotten into you, Olivia?"

Olivia's lips curled downward in a grimace. "Dang, I've been hanging around too many frat boys."

As we stepped out of the restroom, our laughter faded when a blood-curdling scream pierced the air.

"What the...?" I hiked up my skirt and flew across the foyer and up the ballroom stairs.

The crowd parted, revealing a sea of stunned faces. The music had ceased, leaving behind an unsettling silence, broken only by a pale redhead standing near the coffin. Overwhelmed with emotions, she clenched her fist tightly against her mouth and let out muffled sobs. I searched the room for Ashton, but didn't see him. An overwhelming dread pressed me forward.

Marcus stepped beside Olivia, his footsteps echoing on the floor. "There's a body in the coffin."

Olivia's face twisted in confusion. "Why's everyone upset over a skeleton?"

Skylar pointed, her face pale and her finger trembling. "It's not the skeleton. I told you this was playing with fire."

I neared the coffin, a frown forming on my face. The air grew thick and suffocating while the temperature dropped around me. It felt like running in water. I zeroed in on the coffin. The polished shiny black paint was marred only by pumpkins stenciled on its base. The lid lay fractured on the ground. Tentatively, I reached out with a trembling hand to poke the man lying in the coffin, and unease gave way to fear. His pale face and blue lips stood in stark contrast to the black tuxedo.

I gasped and cupped a hand over my mouth.

A knife, stained with blood, was lodged in Trent's right abdomen. His vacant, unblinking eyes gazed upwards, glassy and lifeless.

I frantically waved my hand, desperately trying to get Marcus' attention. "Call 911. Everyone back up. Did anyone touch him? The knife?" I was speaking a mile a minute, motioning everyone to stand back.

While searching the crowd of tuxedo-clad frat brothers and their dates, I couldn't shake the knot in my stomach. I'd become well acquainted with them through the Friday night parties. Warren, Connor, Stefan, and Bradley stood around Trent's head, each displaying a unique shade of green.

"Who opened this?" I demanded when they stayed mute, their eyeballs practically bulging out of their heads, unable to tear them away from Trent's ashen figure.

Hesitant and wary, the young redhead extended her arm. "We

wanted... I wanted a pic-picture with th-the skeleton." She clutched her abdomen. "I'm going to throw up."

Ashton materialized next to me and snapped his fingers, the sound resonating in the stillness. "Get her out of here."

Warren lingered on Trent's lifeless, glazed look before gently escorting the young woman away from the casket.

"Nobody leave." I turned around to face the crowd. A blend of grief, anger, confusion, and fear was evident in their shocked expressions.

Ashton took off for the door. "I'll wait by the front door for the police."

I rubbed my hands together and forced myself to think about what my father had taught me as a little girl. As a forensic pharmacist, he had taken me along on some of his cases over the years, much to my mother's dismay.

I racked my brain. Then, like a bolt of lightning, a realization hit me.

"Everyone into the common room!" I bellowed. "There are couches and food to keep us busy. We need to keep the crime scene clear until the police get here."

I desperately tried to kick start their movement, but they remained as motionless as statues, their unblinking eyes fixed on me. So I did the next best thing. I put two fingers between my teeth and ripped the loudest whistle west of the Mississippi River. Many partygoers slapped their hands over their ears and grumbled, but at least they started moving, ambling toward the ballroom exit.

I took one last look at Trent. His tux jacket was slightly open, revealing a glimmering silver flask tucked into his top left pocket. No doubt it was filled with liquor. What was strange, though, was the pattern of blood around the wound. I carefully leaned over the casket and examined where the blade entered his body, and while there was blood on the knife like you'd expect, it hadn't gushed out. His clothes were barely stained.

"Kaitlynn?"

I spun. Hand on my leaping heart, I chuckled nervously. "Bradley. You scared me."

"Are you coming? Ashton says to keep this area closed to everyone."

"Sure, yeah. I'll be right there."

After a final glimpse at the body, I proceeded to the converted commons room to join my friends. Some ladies had traded their fancy outfits for casual street clothes, while others found comfort sitting on their dates' laps, embracing them tightly. Tension hung in the air along with a miasma of whispers.

Olivia settled down beside Marcus on the couch, their reflections visible in the mirror as Skylar anxiously paced back and forth in front of it. Ben stood nearby, his mouth slightly agape in puzzlement as he observed her. Poor guy didn't know what to do.

Olivia curled her finger at me, inviting me to join her on the empty spot to her right. When I sat, she leaned over and whispered, "What's with Sky? She's been pacing since we got in here, and she's not talking. Trust me, Ben's tried, I've tried, even Marcus did. What did she mean we played with fire?"

Skylar kept pacing, practically burning a hole in the carpet. She gnawed on her fuchsia fingernail, mumbling incoherently about curses and karma.

I sighed and shook my head. "I have no idea, but we've got bigger fish to fry. Trent was murdered, but I don't think it's by stabbing."

Olivia jerked her head back in surprise. "But there was a knife sticking out of his side, Kaitlynn. How else did he die?"

Olivia's question captured Marcus's focus, prompting him to turn towards us. Interest flooded his face. And was that a trace of satisfaction I detected?

"Yes," Skylar mumbled, her eyes piercing into mine.

A surge of uneasiness made my skin prickle with goosebumps. I licked my dry lips and asked, "Yes, what?"

When Skylar's cloudy green eyes met mine, I saw a flicker of surprise in their depths. "Satisfaction." She glanced at Marcus, who seemed taken aback at being brought into the conversation, which was getting odd. "Weren't you mulling it over?"

I stared in complete amazement, my jaw dropping. "Sky, I didn't say anything."

She stopped pacing and cocked her head, her eyes glazed over for a moment. "Yeah, you're right, though. He's almost gleeful." Sky turned her focus on a squirming Marcus. "Why is that? We found your fraternity brother stabbed to death in a coffin and you're... happy?"

Marcus held up his hands, the palms of his hands revealing cobra tattoos. "Whoa, now. I haven't said anything."

Skylar bobbed her head as if someone were talking to her. "Okay, but you're still happy about it."

Marcus hopped up with a quick and nimble movement. "I don't have to listen to this. You're all crazy."

I sprang to my feet and jogged ahead of him, placing my hand on his chest to stop him from leaving. "No one leaves the room, Marcus. Why are you in a rush? Do you know something about Trent's death?"

"Nah, man. You're not pinning this crap on me. Trent had loads of enemies, and truth be told, I didn't like the dude, but I wouldn't kill him. That's cold."

Skylar tsked. "It's illegal, but okay."

"Sky," I scolded, my eyes widening at her bluntness. "Marcus, who had a motive to kill him? The police will ask all of us, and your actions aren't looking great right now. We could easily tell them you've acted suspiciously—"

"All right!" He clasped his hands in front of him. "Trent was on the verge of expulsion from the fraternity. He'd made enough mistakes to—"

Olivia snorted. "If you mean accosting women and being an all around dick, then yeah."

Marcus blew out a loud breath. "Yeah, that stuff. Ashton handed him a letter this morning. I guess he thought this was his last night in the fraternity, and he'd live it up."

I dropped my hand from his chest. "Why was he such a jerk to everyone? Why didn't anyone fight back?"

Marcus stuffed his hands in his pant pockets and rocked back on his heels. "That's the million dollar question. Sure, he's rich, but it's more than that. Trent was a chip off the old block, if you know what I mean. He collected... stuff on people."

"Stuff?" I asked.

"Private stuff."

"Blackmail." Skylar squeezed her eyelids shut, turning her head as if straining to catch a distant sound. "He was blackmailing people."

"Marcus, you—"

"All right, folks. I'm Detective Shaw, and these are my officers. We'll be taking statements one at a time. Ladies first, so we can get everyone on their way. Oh, and the fraternity house is officially a crime scene, so you'll have to find temporary lodging. The university staff will assist. They are currently on their way. May I see Krissy Fox, please? Everyone else sit tight. We'll be with you shortly."

CHAPTER 5

*A*shton walked from behind the couch. I hadn't seen him since he left the ballroom. His eyes looked sunken and grave. He pulled me closer, wrapping his hand behind my head and planting a kiss on the top of it. "I'm so sorry, babe."

I hugged him, thankful for the support. "Hey, what did the cops say?" I asked.

I leaned my head back and searched his face. He was tired like the rest of us. "Not much. I led them to the body, and they bagged the knife after taking loads of pictures. I assured them that no one had touched anything after we found Trent, but lots of people touched that coffin, Kaitlynn. You, me, Warren, Krissy, heck, even Trent."

I frowned. "When they bagged the knife, was there seepage?"

Ash grimaced, sticking his tongue out. "Seepage?"

"Yeah, like blood. How much flowed out?"

Ashton tensed and pulled my arms from around his waist. "That's... gross, Kaitlynn."

"Ash, I—"

"I need a drink." He walked off and disappeared into the crowd of his brothers by the bar top opening to the kitchen. With great artistry, the chef had arranged an alluring spread of pastries and pancakes while the mouthwatering smell of bacon permeated the room.

Olivia stepped beside me and placed a reassuring hand on my shoulder. "What was that about?"

I sighed, running my hands over my face, attempting to release the frustration. "Nothing. Hey, did you happen to ask Marcus who Trent was blackmailing?"

Olivia glanced at Marcus, who was huddled with Ashton in line for food. Leave it to boys to be hungry after a homicide.

"It's a long list from what I gathered. Warren, Bradley, Connor... maybe even Ashton."

My eyes widened. "What does he have on Ashton?"

"From what Marcus said, it could be anything from cheating to theft, but that's for any of them. Trent's father is a high-powered attorney in New York City. He's seen it all, and he apparently taught Trent a lot about his wealthy clients and their dirty little secrets. Like his dad, Trent kept a book on everyone he met. For all we know, all of us could be in his book."

My shoulders slumped. I was exhausted, hungry, and irritated. "Let's start with Warren then. What's Trent got on him?"

Olivia blankly stared at me.

"Great." I sighed heavily. "Let's get started before everyone leaves. Like Dad says, there's no time like the present."

I soon spotted the wiry, lanky, black-haired Goliath in the crowd. He towered above his frat brothers. Plus, he was the only one not eating.

I worked my way through the couches and tables to the far side of the room. In a quiet reading nook, Warren ran his finger along the spines of books bequeathed by former brothers. From Shakespeare to Hemingway, they all sat virtually untouched, gathering dust. I itched to get my fingers on their lovely spines, crack them open, and devour them for days on end. Reading had become a favorite pastime ever since dating Ash. During the lengthy nights when the boys were occupied with video games, there was plenty of time to immerse myself in a book.

"*Once we have a war, there is only one thing to do,*" I said to him. "*It must be won.*"

Warren's mouth crooked into a grin. "*For defeat brings worse things than any that can ever happen in war.*" He tapped a finger on each spine until he found the book he was searching for and flipped it open, bringing it close to his nose and inhaling the dusty smell. "You know your Hemingway. Is he a favorite?"

"More or less. What about you?"

A puff of dust rose when Warren snapped the book closed. "There's nothing quite like him."

I held up a finger in question. "Wasn't it Hemingway who said, '*The way to make people trust-worthy is to trust them?*'"

Warren's face lit up with a big, radiant smile. "He did, but I suspect you're not over here to talk about Hemingway, Kaitlynn."

He motioned to the bench with throw pillows next to the bookcase and we both sat.

"Warren, I've been told Trent wasn't much liked. Some have said he kept a black book on—"

Warren thrust up a hand. "I didn't participate. The others were just having a good time. It wasn't like the girls found out about it. Nobody got hurt."

I massaged my forehead and gauged his quizzical expression. "Wait, what are you talking about?"

Warren reclined against the cushions with a hint of wariness. "What are *you* talking about?"

"Warren, I'm tired, hungry, and about ready to scream. So if you're hiding something spill it, or else I'm telling the cops you're the next person to question."

"Okay, okay, calm down. It's nothing. There's a board with all our names on it, and every week we're asked about the number of girls that we… um… that we *do* things with." Warren rubbed his palms on his tux pants and swallowed hard, his gaze anywhere but on me.

"You rate women on how far you go with them? Or you rate women on their appearances? What is it?"

Warren's cheeks burned fiery red. "All of it."

I intently stared at him. Should I be surprised? Probably not, however, it was despicable nonetheless. Even now, in the twenty-first century, we persist in objectifying women as if they were trophies or achievements. When would we ever stop the idiocy?

"Okay, so you rate these women and keep their names in a book. Trent kept the book? Why is that motive for murder?"

"Whoa! Hold on. I didn't kill anyone, and I doubt anyone would over something so trivial."

I lifted a brow and shot him a disdainful glare.

He tugged on his necktie. "Is it hot in here?"

"Warren, think. Was there anything else in that little black book worth killing over? What about other arguments?"

After a moment of deep concentration at a blackened circular spot on the worn carpet, Warren smacked his thigh with such flourish I nearly jumped out of my skin. "Yes! There was an incident with Bradley. It was something about a test, I think. Does that help?"

I rubbed my aching neck. "Sure. Thanks. If you think of anything else, let me know."

"Warren, baby!" A young woman clad in black velvet and sporting vibrant red lipstick sashayed over to him and settled herself on his lap, planting a deep, passionate kiss on his lips. "My little teddy bear." She nuzzled his nose with hers. "Oh, hi, Kaitlynn. I didn't see you sitting there." She wiped smeared lipstick off Warren's lips. "Hey, did you hear? Warren's got an interview at Yale Law. Could you just die? I'm so proud of my Warry, baby," she said, in a babyish sort of way.

"That's wonderful. Good luck, Warren."

I hotfooted it away. Their lovey dovey make-out session made me ill. When I got two feet from my friends, who all hovered around a plate of food on the coffee table in front of the couch, I veered left when I spotted Bradley.

"Hello, Bradley. How are you holding up?"

Bradley had been picking onions out of his scrambled eggs and pushing them to the side of his plate. He barely glanced at me when I sat beside him.

"Make yourself comfortable, Kaitlynn," he said dryly.

"Thanks. What was that scruff you had with Trent earlier about?"

Bradley flicked another onion to the side, his lips drawn in distaste. "What you really want to ask is if I killed him. The answer is no."

Straight to the point; I liked it. Still, he wasn't getting off the hook that easily.

I leaned my elbows against the table and offered him a napkin since his fingers were dripping with grease.

Bradley eyed the napkin before taking it. "Thanks. I think."

"Bradley, I've heard about the grading system you boys have going on here."

He blanched, avoiding eye contact and squirming in his seat, focusing instead on the food.

"Warren assured me that grading women wasn't something to kill over, but he alluded to something that Trent had over you."

Bradley repeatedly opened and closed his mouth before managing to utter, "Warren is a big fat liar."

I cocked my head, a small smile on my lips. "So you don't grade women on their looks and how far you go with them?"

"I... you see, we—"

"Cut the bull, Bradley. Just answer the question."

"We do."

"Now, was that so hard? What else did Trent have over you? What's this I hear about cheating?"

Bradley lowered his chin to his chest, weariness slouching his shoulders. "Nothing. There's a rumor going around that someone's stealing exams and selling them for cash."

"Why did Warren think it was you?"

"It's not," he insisted, sitting up straighter, finally looking me in the eye.

"Why did he accuse you?"

"I don't have a clue. Warren's an odd person. If you're after motive, then I'd look more closely at Connor. They really had it out this morning before you all showed up."

"What was it about?"

Bradley imitated the action of sealing his lips by pressing his fingers against them. "My lips are sealed. Ask him if you're so keen."

I pushed against the table, stood up, and forced a smile on my face, noticing Bradley looking at someone behind me for the third time. When I turned to leave, I caught sight of a well-groomed young man, barely eighteen, sitting alone by the kitchen. He kept dropping his napkins, his fork, and even knocking over the salt, all the while stealing glances at Bradley. When he realized he was being observed, he paled like he'd been caught in a lewd act.

"Who is he?"

Bradley flushed hot pink and searched the room, acting like he had no idea what or who I was asking about. "Who?"

I hooked a thumb in the young man's direction.

"Oh," he said, leaning back into his chair, giving the young man the once over. "That's Declan. He's a pledge. They're not allowed to sit with brothers yet."

"Ah, right. Hazing. How lovely."

I stepped away, but kept an eye on Declan. He and Bradley were connected in some way, but I couldn't put my finger on it yet.

By the time I'd made my way over to my friends and flopped onto the couch, Detective Shaw had returned.

"Kaitlynn Dahl, front and center, please."

I sank into the comfy couch and grunted.

"Kaitlynn Dahl... I don't have all night," squawked Detective Shaw.

I pulled myself off the couch and reluctantly raised my hand. "Coming."

Before I left, I pulled Skylar off to the side and whispered, "Find out what you can about Declan the pledge and Bradley over there. Something's off between them."

Skylar nodded, her eyes sparkling with understanding as she followed my gaze toward Declan. "I've sensed a strong vibe between them."

I gave her a bewildered expression, but the detective's persistent throat clearing indicated that I would have to discuss it with Sky at a later time.

"Great, gotta go."

"Wait!" Skylar gripped my wrist so hard I winced. Her eyes were distant, lost in a world only she could see. "Trent wasn't killed by the knife like you said. He was poisoned."

With that, she released me, and I stumbled a few steps, my legs wobbly. However, I didn't have time to think as the detective barked, "Ms. Dahl, if you require a police escort, I can arrange one."

Usually, that would have elicited a round of "Oh's" from the juvenile boys, but not tonight. Instead, they simply watched me walk the solitary and lonely line toward the detective's impatient form.

"Coming," I said weakly and ambled out, wondering what had possessed my best friend. Unfortunately, I should have focused on my own situation. From the very first words out of Detective Shaw's mouth, I realized I was in dire straits.

"Ms. Kaitlynn Dahl," the detective began, "for the record, did you or did you not kill Trent Dixon?"

Every muscle in my body tensed as I sat ramrod straight in the uncomfortable chair. She'd brought me back to the dreaded ballroom where Trent's body remained, though now people dressed in white jumpsuits swarmed around the coffin.

"No."

The detective and I sat around a table in the ballroom furthest away from the coffin, where a flurry of cops collected samples, fingerprints, and photos.

She smacked a picture onto the table, rattling it with the force. "Is this you?"

I instinctively reached out to grab it.

"Don't touch," she barked.

I jerked my hand back but inched closer, studying it. I felt my heart skip a beat, bile rising in my throat. "That's me, but where did you get this?"

"I'll be asking the questions, Ms. Dahl. Let the record show that the suspect identified herself in the photo."

"The suspect? I—"

"Ms. Dahl, do you make it a habit of giving men half-nude photos of yourself?"

"No!" I exclaimed, my face growing hot. The faces of our law enforcement pinned me to my seat with quizzical expressions.

With no opportunity to ponder, I jerked back when the detective presented three additional photos without warning. "Explain these then." She stabbed her finger at each one.

I was left speechless, tears starting to form in my eyes. "Detective, I can't explain it. I would never take photos like this." Fear crept into my heart, making it difficult to breathe.

"Can you tell me where these were taken?"

Despite growing angrier by the second, I sighed to steady my frayed nerves, knowing it was better to cooperate than look guilty, so I examined the other photos again. Each one had the same background image. All of them, from the stuffed red panda to the framed photo of Ashton, were captured in the same location.

"That's my bedroom, but I didn't take them."

Detective Shaw narrowed her eyes. "Are you sure? Are you telling me you didn't intend to send them to Trent Dixon or anyone else?"

I shook my head vigorously, hands clutched in my lap so hard my knuckles popped. "No, ma'am. I did not."

One by one, she flipped through the photos and directed attention to the writing on the back. "Please read the script."

I gaped at the script, eyes bulging from their sockets, and my skin prickling with a sense of impending doom. My mouth instantly went dry, as if all the moisture had been sucked out as I spoke the words, "I love you, Kaitlynn."

As I stared at the detective's icy stare, a solitary tear dropped onto the table, making a soft pitter-patter sound. "Detective Shaw, I want a lawyer."

CHAPTER 6

*D*azed, I made my way into the common room, clumsily tripping over a chair leg and barely avoiding a face plant. As soon as the door opened, Skylar's head shot up and she rushed towards me, throwing her arm around my waist and gesturing for Ashton to come over.

"What happened?" she asked in a hushed tone.

Detective Shaw's voice echoed. "Bradley Roberts is up next," sending shivers down my spine.

I jumped at the sound of her voice, and Ashton's face crinkled in concern. "Here, take a seat."

He motioned for everyone to vacate the couch with a flick of his wrist, and I sat on the edge of the couch cushion, folding my hands in my lap. After the door closed, I leaned in and pressed my elbows against my thighs, hanging my head.

"There are pictures," Skylar stated.

Lifting my eyes to meet Skylar's, I could hear the vertebrae crack along my neck. Her bright green eyes shimmered like fireworks.

I brushed away a tear from the corner of my eye.

"They think it's you," she stated.

The room buzzed with whispers as the information spread. Krissy

Fox came over and gave me a comforting back rub, reciprocating the kindness from earlier.

"It doesn't make any sense," said Krissy. "You didn't give Trent any attention whatsoever. Poor Trent. Who would be capable of doing such a thing to him? Everyone liked him."

I, along with Skylar, Olivia, Ashton, Marcus, and Ben, openly stare at her.

"Anyway," Olivia said, tearing her gaze away from Krissy. "What's this about a picture?"

"Pictures," I corrected. I tugged at my hair, rolling a few strands around my index finger. "Somehow, there are half-naked pictures of me in Trent's possession."

"That's insane." Skylar snorted. "You're as prudish as a minister's wife."

I smirked at Skylar. "I'm not *that* bad, but no, I don't take naked photos of myself and send them to anyone."

"So how did he get them? Are they doctored? AI is pretty good these days. If they can mimic actors' voices and faces, then why not yours?"

Doctored photos hadn't crossed my mind, and my hopes briefly rose before plummeting again.

"Except my stuffed red panda and a framed picture of Ashton were in them. How was that done if not from my own bedroom?" I leaned back onto the couch, resting my head against it and closing my gritty eyes.

How did anyone take a photo of me? The only people I allowed into my bedroom were Olivia and Skylar, and they would never do this to me. Even if they did, why give them to Trent? They'd never met him until tonight. Nothing made sense. I mentally reviewed the photos, noting the angle. If I constructed my room correctly, then the photos were taken from close to the television cabinet, but the only thing on that was the TV and the—

My stomach twisted, and the room began to whirl around me.

"Kaitlynn?" Skylar's voice sounded tense, but like she was in a wind tunnel.

I felt someone shaking me, and the room faded into darkness. His eyes, those gorgeous blue eyes that I had daydreamed about and completely surrendered to for the past eleven months, stared into mine. There was a profound sense of sorrow and regret.

"Why?" I asked.

My body was numb. Rooted to the seat, thinking became challenging under the weight of emotions. The possibilities were running wild in my mind. I hoped for any evidence that would exonerate him, but when Ashton stepped back, shaking his head in either fear or disbelief, it only made the ache within me intensify.

Skylar, Olivia, and the rest of the group released their hold on me and directed their attention to Ashton.

I struggled for breath, my heart squeezing tightly. I pressed my sweaty hand onto my hot cheeks and shut my eyes. My voice strained and shaky, I choked out a feeble, "No."

"Ash?" came a female voice.

I opened my eyes. Victoria's presence beside him caused my throat to constrict. Her gaze darted between him and me, unable to decide where to focus. "What's happened?"

Ashton rounded on her, his face contorted in anger. "You did this," he hissed. "Not me."

Ashton angrily wiped his wet cheeks and stormed off to the kitchen, forcefully opening the door and vanishing inside.

"You?" Olivia pointed at Vic. "You did this? Why?"

I hung my head, the weight of exhaustion pulling me down. "Because she's in love with him."

"Holy crap." Olivia handed me a tissue. "You've got some nerve, Victoria."

"Victoria?" Victoria's ex, Jamie, stepped forward behind the couch, causing Amber to release his hand. "You begged me to let you into Ashton's room. Was it really for his birthday? What were you actually doing in there?"

Victoria wrapped both her arms around her waist and backed up, looking small. "Ashton's always been it for me. I'm so sorry, Jamie, but he's what I've always wanted."

Jamie roughly ran a hand through his disheveled hair, strands sticking out in all directions. "Why date me? Why put me through all that, huh? I did everything for you. Flowers, expensive dinners, hikes in the mountains, heck, the trip to Paris... I brought you the world, and you do this?" His face, typically sun-kissed and bronzed, was reddened and twisted with grief. "I loved you. I—"

Vic took a step. "Jamie, listen—"

"No!" Jamie barked.

Victoria flinched.

"You don't get to tell me anything other than what you were doing in Ashton's room that night? No more lies, no more excuses, Vic."

Tears cascaded down Victoria's cheeks, and in a way, my heart broke for her too. From the moment I met her, I'd noticed the lingering glances at Ash. She would always volunteer to go on food runs with him, watch the football games that only he wanted to see, and she was the first in line to organize mixers with her sorority and the Alpha Pi's. She was always by his side, getting him water bottles, a napkin, a cookie. Yeah, I'd seen it, but I ignored it because I too was in love with Ashton. Although, while Victoria was responsible for giving the revealing photos to Trent, she didn't take them.

I heaved myself off the couch and trudged after her. Her hands were pressed against her face, her body convulsing with sobs. As I approached, she shook her head, but I opened my arms wide and embraced her, letting her wail into my shoulder until she was spent.

"It's okay," I whispered to her. "I know. It's okay." I rocked her, stroking her hair.

She finally pulled back and wiped her eyes. I motioned for a tissue, and Olivia handed her one. She blew her nose and gaped at me. "Why are you being so nice to me?"

I smiled. "Anger is so exhausting, don't you think? I always find kindness a better option."

"Excuse me," Jamie interrupted. "She hasn't answered my question."

I brushed Victoria's hair behind her ears and wiped her damp face with another tissue Olivia handed me. "She wanted a keepsake, right? Something of his that smelled of him?"

Victoria's eyes went wide.

"Instead of a keepsake," I went on, "she found the photos."

Jamie scratched his head, trying to piece everything together. "But if she didn't take the pictures, then..." Jamie's mouth formed an "o" shape.

"I'm so sorry, Kati—I mean, Kaitlynn. Trent saw me going through Ashton's drawers and I panicked. He took the pictures from me. I didn't mean for him to have them."

"I believe you."

"So that means..." Victoria paused, then asked, "Did Ashton take the pictures?"

Sadly, it was the only explanation. I wracked my brain, desperately seeking any other scenario, but the angle they were taken from suggested there was only one plausible explanation, and it had nothing to do with my TV.

"Ash gave me a teddy bear a few months back. I set it up on my television cabinet."

Olivia's hand shot to her mouth, her eyes widening in disbelief. "That son of a—"

I held up my palm. "No, I'm just happy there's an explanation. Can someone call Detective Shaw so that we can get this cleared up?"

Victoria took off for the door. "I screwed this all up," she said. "The least I can do is fix this."

The detective arrived shortly thereafter and Victoria told the story behind the pictures. Although the detective was still a bit suspicious of me, she ultimately let me go with a warning. Soon, they had interviewed the rest of the crew, Ashton being the last one. He had yet to come out and from the kitchen and apologize, or at the very least explain why he'd taken those pictures.

Detective Shaw stood at the door while the rest of us looked on. Most of the ladies had put on their street clothes, and we were all ready to head to our homes and sleep. "All right," she said, "everyone can leave except Krissy Fox. Ms. Fox, would you come with me?"

Krissy had been sitting by Connor in the reading nook when the detective appeared. She reluctantly stood, her eyes darting around the room, meeting the inquisitive gazes of all the onlookers. Walking slowly, she kept her arms pressed tightly to her sides. When she finally stood in front of the detective, the room filled with the unmistakable sound of metal clanging.

"Krissy Fox, I'm placing you under arrest for the murder of Trent Dixon. You have the right to remain silent. Anything you say can and will be used against you..."

CHAPTER 7

"Kaitlynn, please!" The handcuffs clicked over Krissy's tiny wrists. "You've got to help me!" she pleaded, her voice quivering. Tears welled up and spilled over her lashes, glistening down her flushed cheeks. "I didn't do this. Call my dad. Call my dad and tell him I didn't do this."

I could only nod, overwhelmed with emotion, as they escorted her out of the room. All eyes were trained on the empty doorway and an eerie silence permeated the room, except for the thumping of my own heartbeat. Then, out of nowhere, Detective Shaw reappeared with a stout uniformed cop to her left, his hand on his firearm.

"Everyone may leave, but we will follow up with some of you," she announced. "If you remember anything, please call, and one of my staff or I will get back to you. Have a good night."

She confidently strode out with the other cop.

Before Detective Shaw's reappearance, people seemed eager to leave based on the hushed murmurs I overheard. Since the alcohol had worn off, a sense of frustration and sadness replaced the joyful atmosphere, and although everyone had talked about leaving, they couldn't bring themselves to get up just yet, remaining in stunned silence.

Olivia puffed out her cheeks and flopped onto the couch, her eyes wide with shock. "Why? I don't get it. Krissy?" Her pretty features twisted in anguish as the motion picture of this evening played out in her mind.

Connor paced the length of the couch, tugging at his hair, his face all shades of red. He tore at his tie and yanked it free, tossing it to the floor. "She didn't do it," he said through gritted teeth. "Trent was a pitiful person, and we all disliked him, but murder? Nah. No way. Not Krissy. I don't care that he—"

Connor stopped in mid step, his nostrils flaring. A wild glint in his eye, he clenched his jaw multiple times, pounding his fists on the couch.

I reached a steady hand to cover his fist. "That he what, Connor?" I asked in a soothing tone. "If you want to help Krissy, then speak up. What did he do to Krissy?"

Connor hesitated to speak when he noticed the crowd and uttered, "Trent *was* a bad person. That's all I'm saying."

With that, he pivoted and stalked from the room. His hasty departure left a void in the room, filled only by the sound of shuffling feet as the rest of the crowd sprung to action, filing out.

With each passing second, the tension faded, as the commons room became less and less crowded. I hadn't moved a muscle, watching the others grab their belongings and leave before I allowed myself to process what had just transpired. A wave of fatigue hit me like a tsunami, and I found the idea of a hot shower, food, and sleep of particular interest, though not necessarily in that order.

I saw Ashton's vacant expression fixated on a spot on the floor. He'd been standing by the full-length mirror we'd used only hours before.

"Ash? Where will you stay tonight?" I asked, after sliding off my heels. The shoes had mercilessly rubbed blisters on my feet, but I lacked the energy to change into my street clothes and shoes. Instead, I stepped into my tennis shoes after putting on socks.

Ashton stood a minute longer, watching me, and then started picking up half-empty plates of food on the coffee table, the aroma of spices still lingering in the air, and carried them to the kitchen counter. Ever since discovering the photos, he had hardly uttered a word to me, or to anyone, for that matter. Even though I longed for an explanation, he obviously had no intention of responding, and I didn't have the energy to confront him tonight. We were both on edge, and a conversation of that magnitude required a filter, which would only happen with adequate rest and distance to clear our heads.

He continued picking up dishes on the outskirts of the room, refusing to even look in my direction. With a sigh, I pulled myself off the couch and walked over to him. He'd stacked five plates of scrambled eggs and bacon when I reached for his hand, the sound of utensils clattering to the table below as I held on.

"Ashton..."

He went rigid, his jaw muscle twitching. He broke free from my hold and clenched his eyes shut, pinching the bridge of his nose. "Don't be nice. I don't deserve it." He ran his hands down his face and groaned.

"Ash, look at me. Please."

He dropped his hands to his sides, his intense stare boring into me. "What?" he barked.

I silently counted to three, my whole body tensing at his gruff response. Who was this person? I hadn't seen this side of him before.

"Do you have anywhere to stay?" I asked, growing more indignant with each passing second. He'd screwed up, not me. His anger was displaced, and I wasn't in the mood to bear that burden.

"Connor's other place. I'm picking up here first, and then I'll drive over." Then his tone changed and he was sweeter, nicer. "Kaitlynn, I never meant for anyone to see—"

"Stop," I whispered, my voice trembling as I retreated. "I can't. We'll talk tomorrow. Get some sleep."

I walked away, never looking back, but I could feel the intensity of his gaze sear into my back. When we entered the foyer, Olivia drew me close, draping her arm around my shoulder, while Skylar did the same on the other side, creating a sense of unity.

"Time to sleep, friend," Skylar said. "Tomorrow's a day for solutions."

We drove in silence to my apartment. In light of Trent's death, we all agreed to spend the night together.

After hot showers, we sat side by side on my bed, our heads wrapped in towels and wearing comfy pink flannel pajama sets courtesy of Skylar. Olivia ripped open a bag of chips with her teeth while I popped open a warm can of soda that fizzed out of the opening and dripped down the side. Olivia sat up and dashed towards the TV stand.

"Oh! That little jerk." In one swift motion, she grabbed the teddy bear, ripped it open, and retrieved a camera. "What a creep."

She dropped the tiny camera to the floor and stomped on it. "That should do it," she said. Then she stalked over to my bathroom, tossed the bear into the trash, and rejoined us on the bed.

"How are you?" She handed me the candy bag, back to her usual cheerful self, and sank her teeth into an enormous Twix bar. "He can't explain himself out of this one. Not this time," she said, crumbs falling onto the bed. She swept them to the floor.

Thrust back into tonight's events, I shook myself forcefully, hoping to rid my body of the overwhelming tension. "I'd rather not think about that."

Skylar leaned over and hugged me. "It's okay, Katydid. What would you like to talk about? Oh, I've got it." Her face lit up like a kid on Christmas morning. "Why aren't you dating Ben? Good grief, girl, he's hot."

"If I were dating Ben, then you wouldn't have a date."

Skylar's full lips turned into a pout. "True."

I let out a small laugh. "No, I'm done with men for the time being. What I want to talk about is Trent."

Olivia and Skylar groaned in unison, collapsing onto the plush king-sized bed. They buried their faces in the pillows.

"Alright, drama queens," I teased. "Krissy *did* ask for our help."

Oliva tossed a pillow aside, sat up, and savored the satisfying crunch of another Twix bar, having gone through the first one. How she kept her trim figure, I'd never know. "No, she asked *you* for help, but—" she wagged the Twix at me for emphasis—"it was only to call her dad, not to go all stealth and track down a killer."

"Who says I'm tracking a killer?"

My friends erupted in laughter. "Right." Skylar patted my arm. "Like you're not?"

"Well…okay, maybe I am, but why not? I won't be sleeping well until they catch the guy. So I might as well focus on something besides nightmares."

Olivia's and Skylar's faces turned serious, their smiles fading away.

"Yeah, I suppose we're not sleeping well either until whoever killed Trent is caught." Olivia said. "What do you have in mind?"

I arranged my fluffy pillows on the headboard, creating a cozy backrest, and settled into a relaxed position beside them, sitting with my legs crisscrossed. "First, did anyone see anything off? With Trent or anyone else?"

Olivia and Skylar were lost in their thoughts.

"Oh!" Olivia's hand shot up in the air. "Trent argued with Warren."

"Who didn't Trent argue with?" I asked. Did anyone like the man?

Olivia went on, her voice filled with determination. "He handed Warren a card or something. Gosh, Warren looked ill, whatever it was."

"Was anything said?" I pressed.

Olivia's brow furrowed in deep concentration. "Trent said something like, 'Best keep it coming. There's more where that came from.' Isn't that what he said to Bradley?"

Wow. It was. So, Trent had a little black book of women, but this was something altogether different.

"Keep it coming," I said, tapping a finger against my leg, and then a realization hit me like an avalanche. "Hey, Trent was blackmailing them." My friends' dubious faces kept me going. "Hear me out. We first see the altercation with Bradley, and Trent told him there's more where that came from, remember? It was a photo. I'm sure of it. Olivia, you remember Trent handing Warren something of a similar size, right? They were both pictures."

Tingles worked along my skin. Detective work was interesting. It was like collecting puzzle pieces, sorting them by color, and fitting them together.

"Okaaaay," Skylar said. "Let's say they *were* both pictures."

"Bradley's was," I interjected.

"If Warren received a picture, and a warning like Bradley," Skylar continued, "then what were they pictures of? Women?"

Olivia crunched on a chip. "But that's not what happened with Krissy and Trent. When I went to the bathroom after Marcus accidentally spilled punch on my gown, I overheard a struggle by the residential wing. When I tiptoed over, I saw Trent pin Krissy against the wall. She put up a good fight and yanked free before I stepped in to intervene."

While she crammed another chip into her mouth, Skylar and I exchanged a brief, knowing glance.

"And?" I asked.

"Oh, sorry." Olivia wiped her greasy hands on her pajama bottoms, leaving a path of crumbs and grease. "Trent said, 'We had a deal.' Krissy told him he was hurting her, but he didn't care. Something like, 'I don't care as long as you pay up.'" She stared at both of us gawking at her. "She yanked free and spit in his face. I wouldn't tick Krissy off. Phew."

Olivia eagerly reached into the chocolate candy bag, her fingers searching for a sweet treat. This time she pulled out a Snickers bar.

"Wow." I exhaled noisily and processed everything. "Trent was blackmailing people."

"That's motive," Skylar pointed out.

"The question is… what was he blackmailing them over? Girls," I tapped my fingers together, "it looks like we need more information. Who's up for a trip?"

Olivia's arm shot into the air. "Oh, me!"

Skylar narrowed her eyes. "Where?"

"Alpha Pi."

Skylar snorted. "You're crazy. Do want us jailed? Or worse…

killed? We know Krissy didn't do it, and that means the killer is still out there. They're probably in that house searching right now."

"That's exactly why we need to act fast. Come on, Sky," I begged. "Pretty please? We'll take our phones and have 911 on emergency dial. We'll stick together, and we'll be in and out as fast as possible."

Olivia wavered her gaze between me and Skylar and shrugged. "I'm in."

I looked over at Sky's pensive face. "Sky?"

Skylar sank into the comfort of the headboard, her lips forming a tight, thoughtful line. "Fine. But we don't split up, and we're out in fifteen minutes. I mean it, Kaitlynn. The second I hear the teensiest creak, we're outta there."

"Deal." I beamed. "Now, here's the plan."

CHAPTER 8

We stayed up until the crack of dawn planning our strategy. After sleeping for a few hours, we beelined for the co-op store and bought black ensembles, including ski masks and gloves. My father had trained me well when it came to fingerprints or leaving any evidence behind. It was a failsafe, and one I took seriously. The last thing we wanted was to be implicated in Trent's murder.

I shuddered, remembering the coldness in Detective Shaw's eyes.

We sat around my apartment coffee table. We'd ordered cinnamon scones from a delicious bakery down the road a block from my apartment. The delivery guy wasn't hard on the eyes either, which was why he knew our order by heart. Plus, we tipped well.

"Kaitlynn," Olivia mumbled, daintily biting into a flaky cinnamon scone, "remind me how we're to get in and out in fifteen minutes? By my calculations, Trent's room plus the ballroom would take on average thirty minutes to process."

Olivia licked her sticky fingers while eyeing my untouched bear claw. I shoved it over to her, grinning when she greedily snatched it.

"We're sticking to the plan. In and out," Skylar said, dipping her glazed donut into her black coffee.

I'd run the scenario on autopilot in my head all morning long, and Olivia was spot on. There wasn't a way to inspect everything in that time frame unless we split up, which I'd promised them we wouldn't.

"We'll make it work," I said, draining the last drops of my chai latte. "If worse comes to worst, we'll only search Trent's room."

Olivia raised a finger. "Forgive me if this one's obvious, but wouldn't the police have confiscated everything already?"

"Possibly," I conceded. "But maybe not. If Trent's the chip off the old block like all his frat brothers say, then there's most likely a hidden compartment they might have missed."

Olivia's eyes grew so wide I thought they'd pop out of her head. "Do you think he's hidden cash? That's what they always do in the movies."

I grinned at her enthusiasm. It lit up her face, replacing the seriousness she wore like a cloak. Her studies meant the world to her. She'd worked hard to get the best scholarships. Med school was in her future, making her the first in her family on both sides to not only graduate college, but earn an advanced degree.

I checked my watch. "Okay. We're leaving in three hours. Let's get dressed and review the plan one last time. If either of you wants to back out, now's the time."

They both steadfastly looked at me.

"Good. Suit up, ladies. We have a killer to identify."

THREE HOURS LATER, and after two more cups of coffee each, we left under the cover of night, parking a block down the road. Raw nerves revved my heart as we crept along the tree-covered sidewalk toward the Alpha Pi house. Thankfully, the city hadn't seen fit to fix the broken streetlamps on the path, which might have been due to the raucous parties for which frat row was notorious. The city deemed it a waste of taxpayer money to keep replacing lights drunk frat boys kept breaking.

The three of us shuffled along, me in the lead, until we reached the yellow police tape hung haphazardly around the front lawn. I crawled under it and motioned for the other two to follow, and we darted behind the building and snuck up the rickety back porch. On the last step, the wooden board creaked and sagged. I leapt to the top like a cat and squatted down, a finger to my lips. Skylar and Olivia's eyes reflected shock and they remained motionless on the bottom two steps. I nervously beckoned them on, watching them carefully step over the weakened board. We huddled by the back door, our hands on each other's backs.

"Remember," I whispered, "Trent's room first. If we have time, then we'll examine the ballroom. Got it?" I dug out a pick to unlock the door.

"How did you do that?" Olivia mumbled in awe.

"Dad taught me," I whispered back, pushing the door open and sticking my head inside. Seeing the foyer was empty, I ushered them in and closed the door.

Since I knew the house by heart, I took off toward the right with only the light from my cell phone screen to lead me. The soft patter of rubber soles followed me through the kitchen, the foyer, and then down the residential hallway, where we took the first left turn.

"This is it." I pointed at Trent's door, now covered by an x-shaped amount of yellow police tape. I stood with my hands on my hips and wondered how we'd enter without disturbing the tape.

Olivia stuck her leg through and contorted into a pretzel to enter his room.

I eyed Skylar in surprise.

Skylar shrugged and stuck her leg out like Olivia, but lost her footing and tumbled backward.

She landed with a grunt, while I bit my lip, trying not to laugh. She wasn't the most graceful being in the world, but this took the cake.

Olivia stuck her head through the top of the x-shaped tape, her forehead scrunched in concentration. "What's taking so long? We don't have much time, and Trent's got loads of furniture to search."

I sobered up and pulled Skylar to her feet.

I stuck my tongue between my teeth and a leg through the opening like Olivia did moments before. Bending over and almost kissing my knees, I ducked my head under the tape and then stood, bringing my other leg through.

"Yes," I whispered, pumping my fist. "Easy peasy."

Skylar planted her hands on her tiny hips and pursed her lips. "My turn."

This time she was through in a beat, and we were searching Trent's room.

All the men shared a room with one other fraternity brother, but apparently not Trent. I guess Daddy's money bought him a private room.

Skylar tiptoed over to his chest of drawers and opened the top one while Olivia was on her knees, searching his closet. That left his desk.

The center drawer slid open without a sound, and I exhaled a breath I hadn't realized I'd been holding. A pocket watch, his passport, and his laptop came into view. I felt along the back of the drawer and turned over the laptop, but nothing else was in it. I moved onto the three drawers on the right side of the desk.

"Nothing in the closet," Olivia hissed while heading over to Trent's bed. She lifted the mattress and searched underneath it.

I opened the first drawer and shone my cell light on it. Drat! Nothing. The second drawer was also empty. When I pulled open the third and final drawer a little too eagerly, something dinged.

"What's this?" I mumbled, picking the object up and spinning it in my fingers.

Skylar craned her neck around, stuffing a rugby jersey into the drawer, her eyes glazed over. "A key. And I know where to use it."

The mattress clunked onto the bedframe as Olivia darted over. Both Skylar and Olivia huddled behind me and stared at the shiny object. It was old, with a finial design on top.

I held it out to Sky. Without hesitation, she wrapped her slender fingers around it, then rapped her knuckles against the bottom of the lowest drawer. A hollow thud echoed in the silent room.

Sky slid her fingertips along the front of the drawer. In one smooth motion, she raised the false bottom of the drawer. We huddled over it, eyes wide in anticipation. A gray metal box the size of the drawer lay underneath, and on top there was a key hole.

Skylar inserted the key and twisted. There was a soft click. She pulled the top off and we all stared at a mound of photographs. The countless pictures of women in various states of undress left me feeling nauseous.

"This is disgusting." Olivia tossed the pics into the drawer and turned away, her mouth in a thin line.

"That's not all." I retrieved a black book from under the pile and stared at it for a moment. Was this *the* little black book the brothers spoke of? Did I want to see inside?

"Well...?" Skylar whispered impatiently. "Open it."

With shaky fingers, I flipped open the cover. Trent's pigeon scratch leapt off the page. The names of women were arranged in two tidy columns. I recognized some of the names from my classes. Each name had a number and either an x or a check mark next to it.

I grew increasingly angry as I flipped through page after page. They dated as far back as three years prior when Trent was a freshman.

"Guys..." Skylar's voice was off. Distant.

I looked up from the page, and the sight made my blood run cold.

"Is this who I think it is?" Skylar handed over the photo.

Olivia crept over, her arms wrapped around her abdomen. "What?"

"Yeah, that's Professor Fletcher." I licked my dry lips and stared at her pretty face. She was an algebra professor, specializing in engineering, but being the junior professor, she'd gotten the lower classes. I remembered her talking about it one time after class with one of her young admirers. Everyone admired her long black hair, pale skin, and bright blue eyes, yet it was her slim waist, ample bosom, and curvy bottom that made the guys go crazy.

Olivia grabbed the picture and stared at it in shock. "No way. A professor?"

I pinched the bridge of my nose. "This just got a lot more interesting. There are hundreds of them. Any one of them had a motive to kill him."

Skylar stuck her hand in the drawer and held up a wad of cash. "Yep, but did these women know he had photos of them? It's not like they're completely undressed. Some are in bikinis while others are fully dressed, and most of them are far off like he was in the bushes snapping shots of them unawares. What's the problem?"

Looking at Trent's small black book, I noticed a few names that appeared multiple times. "Perhaps these names and the photos correlate."

Olivia and Skylar's faces were pensive.

"Hear me out." I pointed out a particular name listed on several pages, and it was always by Trent's name. "What if this is a listing of fraternity brothers and their conquests, but for Trent it was something more? The others had to get pictures of them as we've seen in his drawer. They wouldn't get points unless they handed over a picture. However, in Trent's case, what if he went further? What if he held dirt on these particular women?"

"That's messed up." Olivia crossed her arms.

"I don't disagree. Let's gather up as much as we can and get to the ballroom." I glanced at my watch. "We've spent ten minutes in here already."

"No." Skylar's voice was steely. "Let's split up. We can cover more ground that way. We're not letting Krissy go down for someone else's dirty deed."

Skylar was stuffing the pictures and wads of cash into a pillow case she'd gotten from Trent's bed.

I tried to talk her out of it. "Skylar, we—"

She held up her palm, closing my mouth in a snap. "No, Krissy and all these women are victims, and I won't stand for it."

I turned to the last page of the book and nearly threw up.

"Kaitlynn?" Olivia's face twisted in concern. "What's wrong?"

I raised the picture, and their confusion changed to shock.

"He kept a picture of Krissy?" They asked in unison.

I swallowed nervously, bile scorching my throat, and held up the second photo.

"Kaitlynn..." Skylar's voice shook with fear.

My legs trembled as I heard the blood pounding in my ears like a swarm of bees.

"That's it." Olivia snatched the photo out of my hand and dropped it into Skylar's now bulging pillowcase. "Let's split up and meet at the back porch door in ten minutes."

"Olivia—" I started.

"No." Olivia violently shook her head and stalked for the door, stepping through the police tape. "We're getting to the bottom of this. Don't worry, Kaitlynn. We'll uncover the reasons behind Trent keeping both Krissy's and your photo in his black book. Now go. We're wasting time."

CHAPTER 9

Olivia disappeared into the dark, headed toward the foyer, while Skylar insisted on staying in Trent's room. She remained adamant in her belief that we overlooked something, and with too much time passing, I chose not to argue. I slid through the police tape and decided to investigate the other frat rooms. After all, someone killed Trent, and in my mind, one of the brothers was the likely suspect.

With each creak under foot, I hesitated, hand to my beating heart. These old houses announced people well before seeing them, but in this case, it could work in my favor.

Along the corridor, I peeked into each room, wrinkling my nose as some smelled more foul than others. Just two doors down, the handle jiggled and opened. I bent and eyed the lock.

Huh. Scratch marks appeared around the keyhole and a part of the door had been nicked.

I stepped inside. Illuminated only by the faint glow of my cell screen, the room bore a striking resemblance to Trent's, with the addition of a circular bed covered in red satin sheets and a black fur comforter. Red drapes hung from the ceiling, encircling the bed.

A clever design for a man's lair, but a huge red flag for any female

DEATH ON FRATERNITY ROW

with a lick of sense to turn tail and run. This room lay in utter disarray. The sheets were haphazardly draped over the foot of the bed, some of which lay on the floor like they'd been ripped away. Open drawers had clothes sticking out, with some piled on the floor, and the closet had been completely ransacked. I'd have dismissed it for the police search, but they'd only touched Trent's room, and this was ten times worse.

I bunched up my nose.

Ugh. A chloraseptic odor permeated the room.

I struggled to see anything in the darkness. The bed filled a large swath of the space. The desk and chest of drawers sat side by side on the left wall crammed next to the closet. In contrast to Trent's room, however, a fireplace adorned the right wall, and above it sat a mantle adorned with science and sports trophies. Above the mantle hung a framed portrait of a well-endowed female anime character.

I walked up to the mantle and inspected the trophies, a smirk tugging at the corners of my mouth.

"Warren's a player," I mumbled.

I took a step back when I got a whiff of soot. Squatting, I examined the burned logs leaning closer after seeing the charred remains. Several singed photographs lay on the furthest logs, and as I carefully lifted them out, noting the present heat, I shook them off and realized most of them were too far gone. Except for a few arms and legs, there wasn't much left.

I surveyed the room and absorbed every corner that I could. Once satisfied I was alone, I stood and approached the desk. Since my cell battery was fading, I flipped on the desk light and studied the photos. One was so burned that only an arm stood out, but there was a distinctive mark. I bent closer, my eyes widening in surprise. A tattoo?

I skimmed through the rest of the charred remains and once again came to a stop. Another tattoo, this one of a dragon with a blue tail, was on someone's lower back.

I pressed my hands onto the desk and questioned the motive for burning these pictures. First the forearm with snakes, and then the dragon. They weren't on the same person either, because the hairy forearm was muscular and wide like a man's, and the lower back definitely belonged to a female. The waist was slim and curvy.

The only other burnt object was a scrap of paper so far beyond saving or deciphering except for "letch" that I made out.

I rummaged through Warren's drawers. I didn't find anything out of the ordinary, except for a load of ziplock bags which, on the surface, seemed odd, but when I searched his closet, it made more sense. He had crates full of them, each filled with neatly pressed underwear and socks.

"Wow."

While I'd met loads of tidy people, this bordered on obsessive. No matter. It helped keep the scorched pics and paper safe. Sliding them into a baggie and sealing it, I stashed it in my jacket pocket. However, as I started walking towards the bed, I abruptly stopped. On the expensive rawhide rug I noted soot and... a boot print?

I maneuvered my way across the floor, careful to step around the footprints. The smears stopped next to the bed. Beside it was a trashcan full of empty fruit-flavored vodka bottles and candy bar wrappers, but there was also a discarded prescription bottle.

I retrieved it and studied the label. Spironolactone?

I pocketed the empty pill bottle for later assessment and dug through the rest of his trash.

What was this? I rocked onto my heels and picked out pieces of paper. Matching them together along the ripped seams on top of the bed, I pieced together a letter of sorts full of scribbles and strong language. It spoke of unrequited love and the pain of it, the longing and wishing each day would wash them of the memories. However, it wasn't addressed to anyone. It had to be Warren's writing since, after all, it was his room, yet from what I'd seen earlier, his girlfriend and he were besotted with each other. So why was this letter torn into pieces and tossed in the trash?

I rooted through the remaining trash and didn't find any more burnt pieces. The unexpected beep from my cell phone caught me off guard. It was time for me to meet up with my friends. After retracing my steps, I made it to the ballroom where I found both Olivia and Skylar. I breathed a hefty sigh of relief.

"Hey," I whispered. "Find anything?"

Olivia shook her head; Skylar's unusually pale complexion left me on edge.

I laid a hand on her shoulder. "Are you okay?"

She shook her blonde head. "Nothing about this is okay, Kaitlynn. It's just so tragic. Why stab him? Why not turn him into the police or at the very least report him to the university administration?"

We stood in front of the coffin, which oddly hadn't been taken by the police.

"Maybe they felt trapped. If Trent was blackmailing them like we suspect, then they stood a good chance of consequences too."

Olivia wrapped her arms around Skylar's neck and brought her into a tight embrace. "It'll be okay, Sky. It's time to leave." She and Sky walked off. "Kaitlynn?" Olivia called over her shoulder.

I was too absorbed in the coffin. Something wasn't quite right. "Hang on."

Olivia and Skylar turned to observe the coffin a few feet away.

"What?" Olivia asked. "Did you find something the police missed?"

I asked, "Guys, where's the blood?"

Their bewildered looks returned my gaze with empty expressions.

"What blood?" Skylar asked.

"Exactly."

I rounded the coffin for a better look. "There's no blood. " Don't you see? If Trent was stabbed to death, then why isn't there blood? It would have seeped out of him and onto the sides and bottom of the coffin, but there's nothing, which means Trent was already dead before someone stabbed him."

Skylar's face lit up. "Oh, wow. So what killed him?"

I shook my head. "I don't know, but Krissy didn't kill him with a knife. The cops have it all wrong."

"Great," Olivia called out already hightailing it toward the ballroom exit. "Let's get out of here because—"

In the distance, the unmistakable sound of glass breaking echoed.

"Someone's here!" Olivia's face crumpled into fear.

CHAPTER 10

"Quick!" I hissed. "Behind the coffin."

We scrambled around it and huddled low to the floor, straining our ears for the slightest sound.

Painful seconds, then minutes, ticked by with only the sound of footsteps fading in the distance.

Olivia's saucer-like eyes gawked back at me underneath the moonlight.

"Skylar?" I whispered. "What are you doing?"

She shushed me, her finger to her lip, and poked her head around the corner. "Come on."

In a bent position, she disappeared around the coffin, which left Olivia and me chasing after her.

Following her lead to the ballroom door, it was like the proverbial mice scurrying up the clock as we darted for the exit. We huddled by the door and peeked into the dark. None of us dared to use our cell phone flashlights.

"Okay," I whispered, hearing the quiver in my voice. "There's not too much broken glass."

Olivia and Skylar gaped at me, their foreheads creased in wonder.

"How can you see that?" Skylar said. "For me, it's black, black, and more black."

"Yeah," Olivia piped in, "I can barely see the third step down."

A small grin spread across my face, and I pointed at my eyes. "Viking. We have excellent night vision. My dad mentioned something about more cones than rods in our eyes. Or was it more rods than cones?"

They both shook their heads.

"On my count," I said, "make a run for the door. Whoever is in here left it wide open."

Skylar humphed. "Kaitlynn, we can't see, remember?"

"Then follow me. Ready? One, two, three!"

I flew down the stairs, their footfalls behind me. It took around five seconds to reach the door, but it felt like an eternity.

The crackle of broken glass crunched underfoot, but I kept running. Head down, I pumped my legs, only stopping to check on my friends who about bowled me over.

"Go, go, go!" I stepped aside and allowed them to pass. The glow of the moonlight provided enough visibility and they passed by me without even a glance.

Once on the lawn, Skylar and Olivia kept running, this time at full sprint, while I strained to keep up. Lungs burning, legs screaming in protest, we ended up back at the car a block away, tired and sweaty.

I clicked the car keys and unlocked the doors. They climbed in and buckled up while I trudged around the car, a hand on my side and breathing shallowly against a hitch in my side. My legs protested as I lifted one, then the other, into the driver's seat and buckled up.

"I really need to start running."

A strangled giggle came from the backseat. It took all of two seconds before the car was brimming with laughter.

When we calmed down, I started the engine and drove off, not caring where we went. We'd made it, and that was all that mattered. After a few minutes, I parked the car in front of a pink neon sign and shut off the engine. I faced Skylar in the passenger seat and Olivia in the back.

"Guys, I'm so sorry. That was foolish of me to involve you in any of this. I could have gotten you killed, and that's a mistake I won't make again. Promise. Do you forgive me?"

Olivia reached out and patted my shoulder. "We knew it could be risky. This isn't on you, Kaitlynn."

"Olivia's right," Skylar said, squeezing my sweaty palm. "Don't blame yourself, alright? Now, I'm assuming you want donuts, considering we're parked in front of Gerry's Donut Shop. Let's grab a dozen—"

"Or two." Olivia giggled, propping the backseat door open and hopping out.

She was nearly to the door when Skylar and I took one look at each other and burst out laughing.

"How does she not gain an ounce of weight eating like that?" I marveled.

Skylar shrugged.

"She's got a metabolism of a horse."

We entered the empty 24/7 donut shop, ordered our dozen, and picked a table in the far left corner. The huge floor to ceiling glass windows were smudged with tiny fingerprints and chocolate streaks I imagined left from some curious toddler. Headlights shone every so often from the few cars that drove by as we all sat in silence waiting for our order.

I smacked a hand over my belly, its grumbly protests loud and clear. Scents of powdered sugar, cinnamon, and chocolate churned my stomach into overdrive.

"Ladies." A squatty, fortyish man, with a balding head, big black glasses, and a beaked nose waddled up to our table, setting down our steaming cups of coffee. As he bent, his belly bulged between two buttons, straining against his wide girth. "You're out late."

His smile was warm and friendly, exposing yellowed and crooked teeth.

"I hope the men are treating you well tonight. If not," he stood, flattening the serving tray against his rounded abdomen, "you can always come here. Brent's the name, and donuts are my game, but knuckleheads are plenty on a college campus."

We dubiously looked at his unkempt frame, to which he added with a grin. "Not me, mind you. My son Barry is a former heavy-weight champion, and we don't like men behaving badly if you get my meaning." He turned and waddled back the way he'd come from behind the counter, calling out, "Anyway, your order will be up shortly. I'll send Barry out. One of you he'll like."

The stout man disappeared into his kitchen.

"I don't even want to know who Barry's type is," Olivia said, cupping the hot mug with both hands.

I leaned closer and lowered my voice. "I found something. Maybe."

The chloraseptic smell, the charred pictures, and that torn-up love letter...my gut told me it was somehow all related.

Olivia sipped her scalding coffee while Skylar dumped at least five creamers into hers.

"There's a room down a ways from Trent's, and the door had been jimmied."

Skylar snorted. "Someone's been watching too many old-fashioned cop shows."

"It was ransacked. Someone had burned pictures in the fireplace. The wood was still glowing orange in places. I swiped a few out." I dug the baggie out of my pocket. "They're only remnants, but from the body parts visible, there are tattoos."

I laid them on a napkin and pointed at the bear and the dragon.

"Wow. Unless Krissy had an accomplice, she couldn't have done that, being locked up tighter than a drum." Skylar stirred her coffee.

"Why burn them? Those in particular. Did they not know of the others?"

I pulled out the torn pieces of paper and arranged them until they all fit together.

"This is a love letter," Skylar said.

"No." Olivia read the upside down script. "This is a breakup letter. Whoever wrote this was tormented. Unrequited love? That could be our killer."

"Ladies." A well-built man whose biceps were bigger than my thighs set down our box of pastries with a wad of napkins. The young man, who looked to be late twenties or early thirties, sported a tight fitting pink polo shirt with a dagger tattoo on his forearm.

Skylar stopped stirring her coffee and immediately fawned. She opened the box of pastries and bit into one, licking her full lips. To my amazement, however, he was fixated, not on Sky, but Olivia.

"What's your favorite?" His voice was husky, like he'd been hollering for hours.

"Olivia?" I prodded when she showed no signs of answering.

Too deeply entrenched in studying the letter and photos, she failed to notice.

I kicked her leg hard under the table and she flinched.

"Ow." She rubbed her shin and glared at me. "What's that for?"

I peered up at the man. "He asked you a question."

"Wh-what?" Olivia's rosy cheeks got redder.

Skylar's lips twitched upward. "Ah, she likes bear claws. Isn't that right, Olivia?"

Olivia pushed her mug away, her gaze anywhere but on the man who was unwaveringly focused on her.

"Bear claws are delicious, but I find a danish covers all the bases." Barry picked up the pastry and extended it toward Olivia. "It's a pastry for the masses. The sweet bread leads to a delicious center filled with whatever you want. From custard or lemon to strawberry filling, the possibilities are endless." Barry's fixed gaze held Olivia's unsure stare.

She hesitantly took the pastry, offering a weak smile. "Th-thanks." Olivia set it on a napkin, her ears turned crimson.

Barry tore his gaze from her and studied the pictures and letter. "You're after a killer? Is this some college class?"

"Uh," Olivia tried, but I interrupted.

"Yes." I beamed. "Are you interested in mysteries, Mr....?"

"Barry, and yes. I imagine myself quite good at detective work."

Olivia's shoulders slumped and she caved in on herself. She never saw herself as attractive, and it was clear she wasn't used to such interest.

The chair legs screeched on the worn tiled floor as Barry pulled one over from the adjacent table. He placed the back against the table's edge and straddled it, resting his burly forearms on the chair back. "Are all three of you in this class?" he asked, his steady gaze on Olivia.

"We are," Skylar piped in, all too eager to watch our friend wither under this man's intense interest. "Olivia's the best of us."

"I wouldn't go that far," Olivia mumbled, her voice uncertain.

"She's too modest." Skylar glanced at Olivia. "I bet she'll have this figured out in no time flat."

"Probably so," I said, noting Olivia's downcast gaze and rigid posture. "Still, we'd all be grateful for a little help."

Barry picked up a burned picture and studied it, his brow. "Your professor goes to a lot of trouble for authenticity's sake." He wiggled the photo and soot floated to the table. "This tattoo, though. The dragon is common among lots of people, and so is a bear around these parts." He pointed to the other tattoo photograph. "However, this dragon..." His eyes narrowed. "This one is different."

"How so?" I scooted forward and took another look at it.

"Do you see these details? That's intricate, and most tattooists aren't this skilled in these parts. You'd need to visit Denver. No, this one can only be done by one person." Barry handed the photo over to me. "Visit Ink Well and ask for Lou."

Barry stood and replaced the chair to its rightful table. He grabbed a napkin, pulled out his pen, and scribbled something then handed it to Olivia.

"If you ever find yourself in need of pastries or would like to discuss pre-med, don't hesitate to give me a call."

Olivia's eyes widened. She forgot her shyness and boldly stared up at him. "How did you know I was in pre-med?"

Barry flicked a finger at her wrist. "That's an original, no?"

Olivia tucked her hand under the table. "It was a rash decision."

"You've got talent, but stick to the books. It's a better payoff." He winked at her and walked off. "Have a good night, ladies." He rounded the glass showcase of donuts and gave a mock salute. "If you need a bouncer, you know who to call."

Barry disappeared behind the kitchen door as Skylar and I stared at Olivia's shocked expression.

"A tattoo?" Skylar reached under the table for Olivia's wrist, but she jerked it away.

"I was drunk."

"You?" I asked in surprise. "When?"

"Prom. My date dared me, and like an idiot, I did it. They all laughed at me the next day, and my parents practically killed me."

"Let's see it." I stuck my hand out, wiggling my fingers.

Olivia reluctantly held her hand out. On the inside of her wrist, there was a simple black caduceus.

"How have we not seen this?" Skylar's mouth dropped open as she traced a finger along the symbol.

Olivia shrugged. "I usually cover it with makeup."

"Why?" I asked. "It's quite good. Did you do this yourself?"

"Nah," she pulled her sleeve down and covered it. "I wasn't *that* drunk. Anyway, what did you think about Barry? Should we go see this Lou?"

"Definitely, but first..." I eyed the remaining pastries. "Let's eat." I grabbed a powdered sugar donut and bit into it. A gooey, warm drizzle hit my chin as my tastebuds ignited. "Ummm." I licked my lips and swiped my finger against my chin. "Custard."

"Alright," Skylar said in a chiding manner, "eat up, but then we're after this Lou. Maybe he can identify at least one of the people in the photos."

"Yes," I nodded vigorously, licking my finger, "and then it's off to catch a killer."

CHAPTER 11

The tattoo shop was in a crumbling brick building sandwiched between two boarded-up stores. The glass had been broken on both storefronts, and some of the bricks crumbled into the alley beside it. The facade displayed extensive cracks, and an obvious effort was made to fill them. However, it ended up enhancing the bleakness, a feat not easily accomplished.

I swallowed the apprehension that had crept into my bones, squared my shoulders, and opened the blackened glass door. The black paint had the shop's name, Ink Well, scratched into it.

The bell chimed above our heads and Skylar, Olivia, and I filed in. The door closed, and the fluorescent lights flickered along with the buzzing machines. A blast of cigarette smoke hit us full on, followed by a lingering wave of body odor. Two heads swiveled in our direction, their tattoo machines hovered above body parts. Apparently Sunday was a popular day to get inked. The lobby, consisting of four chairs stuffed against the wall, was currently full. Judging from the reddened eyes that bored into us from the occupants of those chairs, our type wasn't the usual sort to grace the premises.

"There's a two-hour wait," a lean man with tattooed sleeves said gruffly. His tool hovered over the small of a woman's back, exposing the uppermost part of her derriere. "You can wait, but there's standing room only." His voice had the raspy quality of a heavy smoker.

"Uh, no." I tentatively stepped toward him.

The wall of hungover college students grumbled, probably thinking I was cutting in line.

The young woman lying on her stomach propped her head up. Her black-lined eyes glared at me. "The buzz is wearing off, *chica*. Wait in line like everybody else or get lost." She flopped onto her belly again, resting her head on her arms.

"I'm not here for a tattoo," I said, noting my friends huddled by the door, their gazes nervously glancing around the room.

The tattooist set his tool on a metal tray with a clang and tugged off his gloves. "You're done." He looked over at a woman no older than eighteen. "Show me your ID. Adults only." He pointed to a sign in front of the cashier's stand.

The young woman scrambled for her purse, her fingers fumbling through it. A wild grin illuminated her face as she held up her license. She stood, tugged at her clinging miniskirt, and walked over, stumbling only twice. She handed over her card and hopped up on the table the other woman had vacated. "Belly ring first, and if you're nice, I'll think about a tattoo on my inner thigh." She pulled up her tank top a little too high, exposing her lacy bra. "Oops." She giggled. "Too much." After lying down, she patted her stomach. "You're welcome."

The tattooist cocked a brow. "For what?"

In a drunken stupor the woman sloppily licked her lips. "For this." She gestured to her flat tummy. "It's an easy canvas. No rolls here."

The man inhaled deeply and turned to me. "Look, I've got a full schedule and—"

"It'll only take a minute. Lou, is it?"

His tattooed forehead wrinkled. "Nah, I'm Sexton." He craned his neck behind him and snapped, "Lou! Someone's here to see you." He faced me again and sized me up from head to toe while I squirmed under his intense stare. "You're the canvas. Sure I can't convince you to get a Chinese symbol? I've got the perfect one." He grinned and exposed even white teeth, one of which had a sparkling diamond on it.

"Uh, no. I'm fine, thanks."

"Suit yourself." He shrugged, cleaned up his tools and got to work on the drunken college student.

I waited over by my friends for another few minutes when a waif of a woman came up, rubbing her hands with a towel. Her long hair had been braided into multiple strands and swept around her head like a snake. It was dramatic, and quite beautiful.

"Yeah?" She smacked her gum and stared at each one of us in turn. "I'm Lou."

My eyes widened in surprise. "Oh, yes." I recovered my tongue in a few seconds. "We have a picture, or rather, pictures, for you to look at."

Lou tilted her head and sighed. "I'm busy. If you want a tattoo, then wait in line with the rest." She tossed her head in the direction of the other three men glaring our way.

"No, uh, we need your help to identify a person."

She narrowed her eyes at me while I fumbled in my pocket for the ziplock baggie. I handed the first picture to her, and she examined it. "There are lots of people requesting dragons. That and Viking mythology."

I handed her the next one. In the brief moment I observed her, her face flickered momentarily. "The bear is also common. Sorry." She handed the photo back and turned to walk away.

"Someone's been murdered."

She stood frozen, then pivoted on her scuffed, black heeled boots. The studded collar on her neck, designed for a bulldog, glistened in the fluorescent light. "Come with me." She spun and stalked off, disappearing behind a door.

Briefly turning my gaze behind me, I motioned for my friends to follow and rushed after her. We entered a stock room with metal shelving full of inks, alcohol bottles, gauze bandages, and a plethora of other tattooing machines and piercings. Once past the loads of shelving, it opened into a kitchen area with a circular table. Lou sat and propped her feet on the tabletop. She took a puff of her vape and exhaled tiny white smoke circles.

This woman was tiny, but she exuded an energy that set my hair on end.

"Barry directed us to you."

Her eyes brightened with excitement. "Donut man!" She exhaled another puff. Skylar coughed behind me; I dared not look away. "He's a good…" She stopped herself and cocked her head. "Your genteel ears would be offended by what I've done to that man."

Heat rushed to my cheeks.

"No." Her laugh was guttural. "Not that. He's got the most beautiful eagle on his back. It took days. I have to say it's my best work. Barry's not my type."

Although I wondered what her type *was*, that wasn't the point of this visit.

"There's been a murder on campus. Alpha Pi."

Lou snorted.

"You know them?" I lowered myself into a chair opposite her, brushing off a piece of shriveled salami and slimy lettuce.

"They're what we call repeat offenders." A white puff of smoke escaped her circular lips.

"Repeat offenders? Did they get multiple tattoos?"

Lou tugged on the end of a purple braid. "No, they didn't, but they brought in loads of drunk women."

"Isn't there a policy not to tattoo inebriated people past a certain limit?" I asked.

Lou smirked, a glint of humor reflected in her brown eyes with flecks of golden amber on the outer parts of her irises. "We do, but Sexton likes green better than the law. We haven't had any complaints, if that's what you're asking. The women leave happily oblivious and the guys drool after them."

I leaned forward and lowered my voice. "What type of tattoos did these women get?"

Lou eyed me with approval. "Not much gets past you, does it?" She lowered her feet to the floor and exhaled a puff of smoke out of the corner of her mouth. "Chinese symbols. The guys told the women the symbols meant beautiful, sexy, or some type of animal." Her eyes narrowed at me as she stuffed her vape in her pocket.

"What were they really?" I asked.

Lou glanced over at the door behind Skylar and Olivia. "The symbols were numbers. If you ask me, they were rating them." She held up her hand the second I opened my mouth, silencing me. "The large chested women, those that were pretty, got eights and nines, but some average-looking females got fives. I've seen it enough over the last four years to figure a rating system out."

Skylar's derisive snort behind me said it all. Even though I couldn't see her, I imagined the pursed lips and taut features that I'd seen on occasion, especially in the presence of lousy males.

"Were there any tens?" I asked, not out of morbid curiosity.

Lou hopped up from her seat and walked past my friends. When I thought she wasn't answering, she turned.

"Yeah, there was one. She wasn't a student."

"Pardon?" I asked, confused.

"The ten wasn't a student."

I frowned. "How do you know? Lots of people take college classes well into later life."

"Yeah, but do they have professor credentials on a lanyard around their necks?"

Lou smirked, exiting the room and taking the air with her.

CHAPTER 12

"*W*hoa." Olivia clutched her gold necklace, in shock. "That's... I don't know. Is it illegal for a teacher to date a student?"

I became familiar with the workings of a university departments years ago due to a scandal at my mom's university. One of the professors was dating a student. My mom had rushed into our kitchen that night fuming. The university didn't approve of such behavior, but since he wasn't directly under her supervision, they chose not to take action. However, if he had been her student, she would have been dismissed. That night in our kitchen, my mom had gotten upset because her friend, a woman, had gone through the same thing years ago and was unfairly fired by the university. "Males get away with everything," my mom had spat out then baked four batches of oatmeal raisin cookies, which we ended up donating to a local shelter.

"No, it's not illegal," I said. "It *is* frowned upon, though. The only exception is if the teacher is dating one of *their own* students."

I stood and strolled past my friends. It couldn't have been a coincidence that Professor Fletcher's picture was found in Trent's secret drawer. My hunch was they were connected. Was Fletcher tattooed by a fraternity guy? More specifically, an Alpha Pi fraternity brother? Plus, why would a beautiful, intelligent woman like her date a student, anyway? She could have practically anyone she desired.

"Come on," I said, ignoring the grunts coming from the slightly less inebriated female on the piercing table.

We walked out into the starless night. Unusual for Colorado.

We got in the car, buckled up, and I drove off.

"Where are we going?" Skylar's voice sounded jarring in my ears. Olivia's curious gaze met mine from the passenger seat, while Skylar's green eyes reflected in the rearview mirror.

"Home. Let's change and get ready for class. There's a professor I need a chat with."

* * *

"CLASS PAPERS ARE DUE ON WEDNESDAY." Professor Fletcher's blonde hair was pulled back into a neat bun. She wore a fitted, white, button-down shirt, which she tucked into her navy A-line skirt. At first glance, she looked professionally dressed, except for the shirt being unbuttoned too low and the skirt being thigh high. "Give me your best eight to ten pages on Einstein's Theory of Relativity. That is all for today."

Professor Fletcher switched off her laptop, and the white screen's picture of a wild-haired Einstein disappeared. While students left, a few frat boys remained behind. She packed her laptop in a bag. Her skirt drew snickers from some, but one person was completely captivated by her.

I shoved my books into the backpack and marched over to him.

"Connor?"

His sandy brown head snapped in my direction. "Uh, Kaitlynn... what are you doing here?" He shut his notebook, and had the look of a trapped mouse.

"That lady is hot, man. I bet she'd rock my world. All. Night. Long."

Three guys wearing Greek logos snickered and playfully slapped each other while Connor glared at them, breaking a pencil in two.

"Shut up," he snapped, getting up and tossing his backpack onto his shoulder. "Buy some class."

Connor's departure left the fraternity guys stunned speechless. In a huff, they stormed out, grumbling about jokes.

I walked along the rows of seats, positioning myself in front of Professor Fletcher, who only became aware of my presence when she accidentally collided with me.

"Goodness." She splayed her hand against her chest. "I didn't see you there. What can I help you with?"

"Can we talk? Privately?"

Her pupils dilated for a split second, but otherwise she remained poised as ever. "Sure. Follow me."

I trailed the rhythmic sound of her heels through the hallway, into the sunshine, and across the parking lot. Some guys paused mid-sentence to watch her walk by, grinning. When we approached a silver two-seater sports car, she slowed her pace.

"Uh, Professor Fletcher?" I asked, confusion in my voice.

She pressed the key fob and the horn honked twice. "Get in," she said, motioning to the passenger side. "I assume this is private enough?" She slid into the driver's seat, shutting the car door.

I nervously got in, and after I shut the door, Professor Fletcher twisted to face me.

"What's so important that we couldn't talk in the open?" Her velvety voice had a trace of firmness to it.

I hadn't thought about what to say after getting her alone. I wiped my sweaty palms on my jeans. "Um, there's really no way to ask this properly. So I'm just going to say it. Were you seeing Trent?"

A flicker of surprise crossed her face. "The young man who was killed? He was a student of mine, yes."

"No, I meant, did you date him?"

Her lips flattened. "How is this your business, Ms. Dahl? No, you know what? Leave."

In a fit of anger, she jabbed her finger at the door, her eyes burning with fury.

I sat still, my hands lightly folded on my lap, absolutely resolute in

73

getting an answer. "There are pictures." She hitched a sharp intake of breath. "Trent kept a drawer of his... conquests. His and his frat brothers'. So I ask again..." I stared straight at her. "Were you sleeping with Trent?"

Professor Shaw flushed red. "Trent was a fling." She stared out of the windshield, visibly struggling to keep her emotions in check.

"It was only once?"

She shook her head as raindrops pelted the roof of the vehicle. "It's all I wanted, but he... he said it had been recorded. After that," she emitted a derisive chuckle, "I don't know. Everything was ruined anyway. Do you know how hard I've worked to get where I am?" Professor Fletcher fixed her tear-laden gaze on me. "I have three advanced degrees, Ms. Dahl, but all they see is this." She raked a hand down her body. "I get all the entry level classes, and trust me, I understand working my way up, but that's all I've been given. Even the departmental chair holds lesser degrees than me, but will I get a promotion? Not if I don't keep my mouth shut, and then, and *only* then, maybe, just *maybe*, I'll get a nod."

"Why not leave?" I asked.

"Come on, Kaitlynn." It was the first time she'd used my name. Ever. "Don't be so naïve. It's like this everywhere. Beauty takes precedence over intelligence with women. This has always been a big boys' club, and I'm the ornament. The arm candy. However, I also didn't want to lose my job. That would make it almost impossible to work again."

Her dilemma was understandable, yet why she did it in the first place was the question.

"I was drunk."

The statement caught me off guard. It was like she'd read my mind.

A smile played around her lips. "Isn't that what you were thinking? Gosh, I regret it all. That boy put something into my drink. Wait. That's not exactly true. He handed me a bottle of water, and I didn't think anything of it. Trent and that other one..." She snapped her fingers, conjuring up a foggy vision, "Warren something or other."

My hands tightened into fists in my lap as a powerful surge of anger hit me, making it difficult to breathe. "He date raped you? Did Warren participate?"

Her trembling breath made my stomach churn. "I should have known better. Trent was a terrible student, and I'd heard the rumors. Warren was a tagalong. From what I remember, he spurred Trent on and left us. Anyway, what's done is done." She reached over and placed a comforting hand on mine. "I'll be alright, Kaitlynn. Take this as a lesson to never take a bottle or glass of anything from anyone, all right?"

"Why didn't you turn him in? Why not call the police?"

The corners of her mouth tugged with a melancholic smile. "It's my word against his, and with his father? I wouldn't win. However, there is something you can do for me. Burn the photo. Burn them all. No one needs to be dragged through this. Will you do that for me, Kaitlynn? Will you do that for all the women he's done this to?"

CHAPTER 13

On the long drive home all I could think of was Professor Shaw's earnest expression, and that question: *Will you do that for me, Kaitlynn? Will you do that for all the women he's done this to?*

I couldn't burn the photos. It wasn't right. Not to say that what Trent had done was okay either, but the law was the law. I'd learned that from my father.

I turned into the alley leading up to the Alpha Pi house. Ashton had messaged that they'd been allowed into the house again. The professor's disturbing remarks angered me so much that I longed for his comforting embrace. I needed him to assure me that everything would be fine and that he was unaware of Trent's vile actions. I needed confirmation from him that he wasn't involved in any of this, despite knowing Trent had those revealing pictures of me.

I trudged up the back porch steps. The yellow police tape draped out of the garbage can at the bottom of the stairs. I raised my fist to rap against the door, then stopped, trying the knob instead. They always left the back door unlocked. Though, after the murder, maybe they'd locked it.

"Nope," I mumbled and stepped into the kitchen.

I mentally replayed the conversation I had with Professor Fletcher while I walked toward Ashton's room on autopilot.

"Hey, Kaitlynn," someone said as I blindly made my way past the kitchen island.

I glanced up. "Oh, hi, Connor."

Since neither of us felt like talking, we simply walked past each other. There were a few fraternity brothers wandering the hallways, their subdued behavior speaking volumes.

As I approached Ashton and Connor's room, I heard a high-pitched giggle coming from behind the closed door. My heart slammed against my ribcage and my palms were clammy. The walls seemed to close in while I stood frozen in place.

I gaped at the door when another round of giggles erupted behind the closed door decorated with a glitter "Welcome Home" sign I'd created at the beginning of the year. It was most definitely female. In Ash's room. I pressed my ear against the door, desperately hoping that what I had heard was not real.

Another giggle followed by a "Shh."

My head snapped back in shock, my eyes widening. I gasped and clutched at my chest, fingers trembling against my racing heart. Waves of fear surged through me, causing my entire body to quake uncontrollably, as if each nerve were electrically charged.

I reached a shaky hand to the cool doorknob. "Please," I whispered, "please be somebody else."

The knob yielded under the pressure of my sweaty palm, turning effortlessly. With a trembling hand, I nudged the door open, pausing at the threshold. As the door swung wide, a rush of dread engulfed me, threatening to suffocate any semblance of courage.

"No," I croaked, tears welling up in my eyes. I turned away, only to be halted by his desperate call.

"Kaitlynn, wait!"

I swiped at the tears cascading down and took off, ignoring the plea, each step a thunderous echo in my heart. The heavy thuds of footsteps pursued me relentlessly as I sprinted into the foyer, my breath coming in ragged gasps. With every ounce of strength, I propelled myself forward, my vision blurred by tears, blindly fleeing past the stunned faces of the Alpha Pi fraternity brothers, their silent stares propelling me on.

I flung open the kitchen door, fueled by adrenaline that pushed me beyond my limits. Disregarding any repercussions, I swiftly made my way through the chaotic kitchen amidst the cacophony of clattering pots and pans, completely consumed by the need to flee. The fraternity house and its inhabitants were mere blurs in my peripheral vision, overshadowed by my urgent desire to run away.

In the dimly lit space, the back door stood as a symbol of freedom. Just as my hopes swelled, a sudden movement to my right shattered my focus.

WHACK!

Intense pain exploded behind my eyes and stars danced in my vision. I crumpled to the ground, limbs trembling with shock and agony, as darkness consumed me.

* * *

"Kaitlynn?" The voice, gruff with worry, sliced through the haze.

My eyelids fought against the weight, struggling to open.

"Kaitlynn? What happened?"

Above me, Ashton's face materialized, his features etched with concern, a clear indication of how grave the situation was.

The world swam in and out of focus as I blinked, my skull throbbing with pain. "Ow." My hand shot up instinctively, fingertips coming away slick with blood.

Ashton's eyes widened in alarm. "We need to call an ambulance."

"No." I pushed myself up onto my elbow, determination warring against the dizziness threatening to pull me back down. I tried to rise, but the room spun violently, making me crash back to the floor again.

Ashton stood behind me and gently pulled me into a seated position, wrapped his hands underneath mine, and lifted me upright. His strong arms pressed me into his hard chest. The room viciously spun in front of me.

I rested my head against his shoulder and shut my eyes.

His lips hovered by my ear as he whispered, "You're okay."

If only I was...

I cautiously opened my eyes and sighed. The spinning had stopped, but several pairs of eyes fixated on mine, awash with concern.

"Here," Connor said, handing me a white hand towel. "For your head."

I took it and pressed it to my throbbing temple, wincing.

"What happened?" Ashton asked again.

I thought back to minutes before when I was running into the kitchen of the Alpha Pi house. The flash of movement. The agonizing pain.

"Someone hit me."

I turned my head slowly to keep the nausea at bay and peered down at the floor. The worn black handle of something stuck out from behind the open door.

"There." I pointed, setting Connor in motion.

"Geez." Connor retrieved the offending object. "Someone hit you with a skillet?" Connor let out a low whistle, holding it up in the air for all to see.

"Baby bear?" A sleepy-eyed brunette walked over dressed in a man's formal shirt, which cupped her supple bottom and exposed the length of her thighs. She smoothed her bed-head and stared up at Warren with puppy eyes. "What's taking so long?"

The young woman glanced over at me.

"Nothing, doll," came Warren's deep baritone to match his enormous height. He strolled over and kissed the top of her head. "Go back to bed. I'll be there shortly."

The girl took one last look at me, then plodded off the way she came.

"Kaitlynn, that's quite a knot," Warren remarked, his voice laced with concern. Retrieving a bag of frozen peas from the freezer, he passed it to me. "Looks like someone's not pleased with you. What were you up to in the kitchen?"

Warren's gaze shifted between me and Ash, his eyes narrowing with suspicion.

Ashton's hold around me tightened, his embrace almost suffocating.

I lifted my head, catching sight of his tense jawline and intense stare fixed ahead.

"Victoria," I breathed out, the name heavy with significance.

Fresh tears welled up in my eyes as I broke free from Ash's hug, finding the courage to stand and make my way to the door.

"I have to leave," I declared, though even as the words left my lips, the room spun and I stumbled.

Ash caught me, pulling me tightly against his chest. My throat tightened with overwhelming sadness. All I wanted was to escape from the weight of it all—the betrayal, the infidelity, the fraternity brothers. I didn't need to see their faces to feel the sympathy emanating from each of them. They were typical college guys, yet they harbored compassion too. The sight in the mirror above the sink confirmed my worst fears. It was my downfall.

Breaking free from Ash's grasp, I dashed away, the echo of my hurried footsteps on the wooden porch steps the only sound piercing the heavy silence.

CHAPTER 14

"*K*aitlynn, wait!"

Faster than a jackrabbit, I took off for the car. With a faint beep, the doors unlocked, thanks to my trusty key fob. I threw the door open and jumped inside, slamming it shut. As Ashton's fists collided with the car hood, the engine roared to life.

"Stop. Let's talk. I can explain!"

His fraternity brothers and girlfriends leaked onto the back porch, staring intently at the scene unfolding between us.

I rammed the car into reverse. I put the pedal to the metal, and the engine squealed against the abrupt propulsion. It jerked backward, smashing into a trashcan full of police tape, knocking it over with a clang. Those on the porch scrambled into the kitchen.

Ashton stood motionless, his hands hanging lifelessly at his sides. "Kaitlynn, please. Don't do this," he pleaded.

Through the windshield, I watched him, feeling the weight of his words. He had been my everything, my reason for living, for nearly a year. I had given him every part of me, every thought, every breath, and he had reveled in it. It was different now. I couldn't bear to continue existing solely for him.

A wave of anguish crashed over me, sending shards of pain

through my heart, making it hard to breathe. "You're not my problem anymore, Ashton," I managed to say, our eyes locking in a silent battle of wills. With determination, I rolled down the window. "I'm done."

I slammed my foot down on the accelerator and the engine roared to life. The tires screeched in protest as I tore away, leaving behind a cloud of dust. In the rearview mirror, I caught a glimpse of him, spinning around to watch me vanish into the distance.

* * *

When I got home, I nearly forgot the head wound. It wasn't until Skylar popped over, a box of donuts in hand, that I remembered.

"Hey, girl. That Barry is a right good man, and if Olivia doesn't want him, then—" Her exuberant face faltered. "What the heck?" she squealed.

She rushed to the countertop and dropped the boxes down, jogging back over to me. She touched my hairline with her fingertips.

"Ow!" Her touch flooded my mind with the agonizing moments of the past hour.

When Skylar fixed me with a hard glare, I sighed and stepped back, a sense of shame tainting my already low esteem.

"Sorry, Sky. I didn't mean to snap. It's… it's been a difficult day."

She dug into my medicine cabinet and drew out the first aid kit. She moved robotically, collecting gauze, a bandage, antibiotic ointment, and a cold compress before she finally turned to me and beckoned me over to the bar stools. She even made a pot of coffee, and I sat with a steaming cup close to my chest while she worked.

"Someone belted you with a skillet? A cast-iron skillet?" Her voice was incredulous, but her expression was all business. "Spill it, *chica*."

Even though she'd showed abilities, I still reeled with how she knew such things. I reviewed all the sordid details, and when I was finished, I studied her face for any semblance of an emotion.

"Huh." She tapped her nail on the Formica countertop but gave no other indication of what she was thinking. "Right." She slammed her fist so hard on the countertop I jumped and spilled the hot drink, mostly on the counter.

"We're onto something," she said. "It's definitely someone with access to the house."

Okay, if she was ignoring the elephant in the room called Aston, then I would happily play along. It was all too exhausting to hash out, and Krissy's plight wasn't any better.

"From what you've gathered," said Sky, "Warren's next on the list. And boy, do I have a bone to pick with him." She balled her fist, her mouth in a straight line.

"Calm down, Hercules." I cracked a grin, feeling a weight lift from my chest. She had that effect on people. "Go easy on him until we've gotten all the information we need. Afterwards, he's all yours."

Skylar cracked her knuckles and hopped off the barstool. Grabbing her backpack, she slung it over her shoulder and headed for the door. "Bring the bear mace just in case. I've forgotten my brass knuckles."

* * *

Once again on the Alpha Pi porch steps, I balked when a fresh round of heartache tore at my core. The hours-old memories made me queasy, but Warren had said to meet him at the house, so here we were.

"Kaitlynn," Skylar's said, "I can do this on my own if you want. You can wait in the car."

It took a second for me to shake it all off. "No, I'm fine." I straightened and pushed past her into the kitchen.

Not much had changed with pots and pans still on the floor from my earlier encounter. Oblivious to the chaos, Connor was bent over the gleaming steel countertops, fixing a peanut butter and jelly sandwich. One look at me, and the knife clattered to the table.

"Kaitlynn?" He rubbed his messy hands on his jeans and left a streak of peanut butter on his hips. "Should you be here?" He nervously glanced behind me at Skylar. "Shouldn't she be at a hospital? She took quite the knock."

I studied him from head to toe, an unease settling in. "How's Krissy?"

"Uh, she's fine." He was acting rather aloof with a girlfriend jailed for a murder she claimed not to have committed.

"What was Krissy arguing with Trent about?"

Connor's head snapped toward me, his mouth hanging open in surprise. "Krissy argued with Trent? When?" He picked up the knife and gripped it tightly. He stepped closer. "I told her he was bad news. I told her to stay away from him."

I narrowed my gaze. "Why?"

The sound was so low that he inched closer with only a couple of feet separating us. Pronounced dark circles under his eyes spoke of someone who hadn't slept. His rumpled garments and inside-out long-sleeve shirt suggested either panic or a lack of cleanliness. Connor usually took pride in his appearance.

"Connor, why should Krissy stay away from Trent?"

He shook his head and turned to walk away.

"We know about the pictures. And the black book."

Connor faltered for a moment, then he hastened to the kitchen door leading into the foyer.

"We know about the numbering and the tattoos," I called out.

Connor froze and turned a deathly white. "We can't talk here. Follow me."

CHAPTER 15

*W*e sat on the edge of Connor's bed across from Ashton's. I stared at the neatly made bed and the divot where two people had been. The memory left an indelible mark on my mind.

Her shirt lay on the foot of the bed, her hair tangled in his hands as she sat astride him, her tight jeans accentuating her firm buttocks. Their faces hovered close together, and her flushed complexion showcased a hint of triumph as she looked down at him.

After shutting and locking the door, Connor cleared his throat and stood in front of us. "No one will bother us." He stated it with a matter-of-fact tone, yet I detected a trace of sympathy in his words and noticed the fleeting glance directed my way. "Trent was a jerk. I told Krissy that, but she didn't believe me."

He began pacing back and forth in front of Skylar and me. We remained silent, waiting for him to resume speaking.

"One day, Krissy came to me. She was crying, and her clothes were torn. I thought... I..." He drew in a shaky breath before continuing. "Trent had propositioned her. When she said no, she saw him pour something into her drink." Connor abruptly halted and turned to face us. "Krissy's lots of things, but stupid isn't one of them. She ran for the door, but Trent's incredibly fast." His face flushed with anger, turning a furious shade of red. "He grabbed her and threw her against the wall. She kneed him and flew out the door. She came directly to me, but I couldn't calm her down. He did something else. Something so horrible she wouldn't even tell me. You've got to believe me. Krissy didn't kill Trent. I'll be her alibi. As a matter of fact—"

Connor snatched his keys off his desk and stormed for the door.

"Hold on!" I stood up from the bed, stealing one final glance at Ashton's sky blue comforter.

Connor paused, his back still turned to us.

"Tell us about the tattoos."

Connor's head drooped and his shoulders sagged. He pivoted, his face awash in guilt. "I didn't agree with it, nor did I go along with it. I tried to warn those girls that—"

"Women." Skylar's stare pinned him to the door. "They are women, not girls."

"Sorry." Connor raked a hand through his cropped hair. It sprang back into place like a spring. "I meant no disrespect." He stepped forward, gripping the keys in his palm. "They wouldn't listen. Trent had a way with gir— uh, I mean, women. Maybe it was his money, or maybe they really liked him. Whatever it was, he got them to do things."

I arched a brow. "Like a tattoo? Was that before or after he roofied them?"

"Listen, I didn't know about that. All I saw was them drinking. That's it. If I had known—"

"You would have stopped it?" Skylar said, a brow raised.

"Yes. Maybe. I don't know." Connor spun for the door.

I wasn't going to allow him to leave without extracting as much information from him as possible. "Tell us about the numbering. Did the women know the tattoos were a numbering system?"

Connor turned to us again, his expression now stoic. "Probably not."

"Did all the frat brothers participate? How many women on campus are marked?"

He winced at the last word. "Over the last four years? Probably a few hundred."

Skylar snorted derisively. "Branded like cattle, and they don't even know it."

"Connor," I snapped, "did everyone participate?"

"No," he blurted. He puffed out his cheeks. "Most did. I'm no hero. What was I supposed to do?"

My body vibrated with anger. "One more thing..." The room grew so quiet the hairs on my body stood on end. "One of the women we questioned mentioned Warren was present when Trent spiked her bottle of water."

Connor's complexion was a sickly shade of green. "Professor Fletcher," he mumbled, his gaze fixed downward as if the floor had transformed into a fiery pit ready to engulf him.

Without uttering a word, he swung open the door and stormed out.

Skylar stepped to the door and peeked out, looking left then right, then walked back to me. "That's not suspicious at all. What's your gut tell you, Kaitlynn?"

With a new view, I scanned the room that had become like a second home over the last year. As much as I wanted to flee, it warranted a further look.

The neat beds butted against their desks, and behind them were their closets.

"What are you doing?" Skylar asked.

Ashton's closet door creaked open when I pulled the knob. The house was built about fifty years prior, and from the moment I'd set foot in it, I'd fallen in love. Although the old closets appeared small in our modern perspective, they carried the scent of bygone days.

I took a deep breath, noticing the dust in the air, but there was an additional presence, something else lingering.

Skylar padded over, the heels of her leather ankle boots clacking on the wooden floor. "Kaitlynn," she sighed. "Ash is a jerkwad of magnanimous proportions, but now's not the time."

I trailed a finger down the sleeve of Ashton's form jacket and twisted the cufflink. I tugged at the other sleeve and pulled it up for a closer inspection. "It's missing."

"What's missing?"

Bending down, I rummaged through his shoes and dirty laundry, then stood up with a grunt.

Skylar watched me curiously as I next searched Connor's closet. On my hands and knees, I pushed books, notebooks, and crates full of neatly folded clothes aside. In the center laid a silver cufflink.

"Why would Ashton's cufflink be in Connor's closet?" Skylar asked from somewhere above me.

I was too busy rapping my knuckles against the wooden slats of the floor. My pulse quickened when a board jostled. I dug my nails between the wooden panels and wiggled it free.

"Holy moly." Skylar's voice rose an octave.

Her shockingly blonde hair fell over her face as she looked down at the hole in the closet floor. "What are you waiting for?" she asked.

I dug out a cobweb covered metal box the size of a shoebox with a combination lock.

"Great." Skylar stalked away and plopped onto Connor's bed. "We'll never get that thing open."

I traipsed over to Ashton's bed and sat with it upon my lap. "Oh ye of little faith," I playfully scolded her, giving her a brief glance.

Skylar regarded me with a smirk as I tried a few combinations with no result. "Give it up, Katydid. It's pointless."

I glanced up at the ceiling, my mind racing through various scenarios, when I sat upright with a start. My small smile transformed into a wide grin.

"Ah," Skylar tsked. "You've figured it out. I've memorized that look."

Counting under my breath, the tension mounting with each number, I twisted the lock mechanism: 2... 3... 2... 3... Finally, a soft click reverberated, sending my heart into a frenzy, pounding against my ribs. With cautious deliberation, I lifted the lid with anticipation.

Skylar hopped up and darted over. She sat next to me and picked out some folded exam papers, a birth certificate, a jade dragon, and studied them while I lifted up a few photographs, displaying a young teenage girl sporting a French braid, smiling at the camera and exposing a shiny mouthful of braces. The young woman resembled someone I couldn't quite put a finger on yet.

I moved it to the bottom of the stack and viewed another photo that showed Connor, Warren, Bradley, and Trent at a math quiz put on by the math department. They posed in front of a "Winner" banner from this past spring. Confetti floated in the air. Trent held up the large trophy while Warren admiringly looked on. To the left of them was the less than thrilled faculty member who'd hosted the event.

I waved the photo in the air until it drew Skylar's attention.

"What?" She snatched the picture and studied it. "The math-a-thon? So?"

I pointed at the professor and her confusion melted into surprise.

"Professor Fletcher? Do you think this was when Trent did his thing?"

I pointed again. Her face wrinkled as she examined it.

"Take a look at Connor," I said.

"He's not happy," Skylar said, handing the picture back.

I shook my head and held it in front of her. "Look who he's staring at."

A faint dawn of recognition flashed within her green eyes. "He's not upset." Skylar's lips tweaked up at the corners. "That's lust."

I grinned. "That's motive."

CHAPTER 16

*J*rapped my knuckles on Warren's closed door and smirked
at the whiteboard.

"Do your damnedest in an ostentatious manner all the time?"
Skylar's voice traveled down the long hallway. "He's no Patton."

The door swung open.

"Hello, ladies. What can I do for you?" He leaned against the door
frame grinning, blocking entry. His black silk robe hung open and
revealed pumpkin-covered boxer briefs. The rest of him glistened
under the light.

I forced myself to hold eye contact, but the body oil nearly did
me in.

"Um, yeah," I scratched my head as I locked eyes with him. "We
have a few questions."

Warren stepped aside and gestured for us to enter with a sweeping
wave. "Mi casa es su casa."

He playfully bowed while Skylar and I remained fixed in place in
the hallway.

Warren's head inclined toward us, his grin growing wider. "I
assure you, I won't bite."

Skylar gave a fleeting glance toward me, squared her shoulders, and walked in.

As soon as I entered the room, a pungent incense assaulted my senses and made it hard to breathe. I covered my mouth with a fist and coughed repeatedly, resulting in a sneezing episode. Skylar, on the other hand, had only entered so far as his desk and perched on the edge of his ergonomic desk chair, folding her hands upon her knees.

Warren loped over to the window above his bed and opened it a foot. "Is that better?" He cast a glance in my direction before stalking across the room toward Sky.

She tensed at his approach, but the second he passed her for his closet, she visibly relaxed.

Warren stepped into a pair of jeans and cinched his robe about his torso before turning to us. "Would either of you care for a beverage? Water? Wine?" He waggled his bushy brows. "Whisky?"

This was a game for him, which in ordinary circumstances would be expected, but since Trent's demise, and those horrid pictures, let alone the tattoos and history of roofies, it landed with a less than enthused response.

Skylar's eyebrow reached toward her hairline. "Plan on drugging us too?"

"No to the whisky," Warren said, unfazed. He whipped out a shot glass, filled it with an expensive brand of vodka, and slugged it. Next, he filled a whiskey glass and poured it full of bourbon. With long, even strides, he walked to his bed and lowered himself in one fell swoop, propping back against fluffy pillows on his round bed.

I marveled at how effortlessly he moved and never spilled a drop of the fancy bourbon. My father was into bourbon, and he'd only partook of this particular brand once. It was when he'd won an award for advancements in forensic pharmacy.

Warren sipped and stared at us over the glass rim. Swallowing, he sighed.

"Nothing beats a good bourbon. You sure I can't tempt you into one?" He waggled the glass, the ice tinkling against the sides.

Skylar pursed her lips. "The only tempting you're getting will be from your lovers. We have more class."

I fought to suppress a snicker.

Warren turned his attention to me. "Seriously?" He fixed me with a pointed stare, sobering my amusement. "I thought you were into sloppy seconds?"

Warren savored a sip from his glass, observing the impact his words had on me.

"Enough," Skylar snapped. "You and Trent liked to drug females, tattoo them, then take their pictures."

If Warren regretted his actions, his expression failed to show it. He raised his index finger, tutting. "I didn't drug the women. That's a whole other can of worms." Warren grinned. "From what I could see, though, they didn't seem to mind. And they weren't in any real danger."

Skylar shot up from her seat. "You son of a—"

"Hey, whoa." I stepped in front of her, blocking her path before she could attack him. Her body trembled beneath my touch. "Don't lay a hand on him," I whispered into her ear as she struggled against my grip. "He'll have you arrested. How does that help Krissy or you?"

Skylar muttered a curse under her breath, her body coiled with tension, though she ceased her attempts to break free from my hold.

Warren's chuckle only served to agitate her further, causing her to jerk once again.

"Let me deal with this, okay?" I snapped.

Skylar jerked out of my grasp, nostrils flaring in anger, but she eventually relented, making her way back to her chair and sinking into it.

I let out a loud exhale and spun to face Warren.

He drained the glass and held it up in the air, his lips in a full pout. "I'm empty. Filler up?"

This was a game. All of it. That much was clear, and if I wasn't in the right headspace, then Warren would be roadkill cookoff in two seconds flat. Luckily for him, I had a plan, and I *always* followed my plans.

Adjusting the hem of my shirt, I rose to my full height. Tilting my head to the side, I crossed my arms over my chest and smirked. "I'm not your maid, Warren. Nor am I one of your girlfriends. But what I am," I took a deliberate step toward him, "is your worst nightmare." I took another step, closing more distance between us. "Unless we get what we came for." With yet another step, I found myself standing by his headboard, towering over him.

The mischievous grin dissolved, replaced by a steely expression, and he set the glass down on his lap. "Warren doesn't respond well to dominance." His voice was low, laced with a threat.

"Kaitlynn," Skylar's voice cut through the tension.

I stood my ground, locking eyes with him, my glare unwavering. "Krissy didn't kill Trent. But *you* had motive."

A rush of warmth flooded my cheeks. I felt like I was clutching at straws, with nothing concrete to support my suspicions except for Trent handing Warren a few pictures at the party—pictures that Trent had also used to intimidate Warren.

Warren let out a derisive snort. "Me?" His swagger returned. "You must be out of your mind."

"Is that so? What about those pictures of yours, Warren? Care to explain?"

A fiery intensity sparked within his eyes. "You know nothing," he snapped, rising to his feet in one fluid motion. Warren loomed over me, and I struggled to maintain my composure.

"Guys," Skylar interjected cautiously.

Her footsteps were muted against the plush oriental carpet.

She clutched my shoulders tightly as I stood fixed in place, glaring up at Warren. Tension radiated from him, as if he were on the verge of exploding with rage. Skylar gently pulled me backward.

It felt like a tug-of-war, and at that moment, we were on the losing end.

We retreated toward the door, maintaining unbroken eye contact with Warren.

The door creaked open, and a rush of cool air from the hallway brushed against my flushed skin. Skylar and I exchanged a tense glance before stepping into the safety of the corridor. Just as we began to walk away, Warren's voice, low and threatening, pierced through the air.

"Bradley's the one you're after, and Ashton. I'd mind your own backyard and leave my sister out of this."

We hurried down the hallway, wincing at the slam of his door behind us.

CHAPTER 17

$\mathcal{W}$e dashed into the foyer, both of us casting glances over our shoulders, when I slammed into a wall.

"Umph!" My hands shot up to cushion the impact. My teeth rattled from the abrupt halt, and I stumbled into Skylar.

"Kaitlynn?" Ashton's keen eyes took me in. The flecks of amber were more prominent in the daylight. "Are you okay?" He looked past me into the hallway. "Did someone bother you?"

I winced at his bruising grip.

"No." I shook my head, exhaling with relief when his hold loosened. Then I remembered I wasn't speaking to him, and why we were in this situation flooded back. I shrugged off his hands and headed for the front door. I yearned to leave behind this dreadful house and its inhabitants. Even after almost a year of practically living with them, I realized you never truly know people.

"Wait."

I stopped so abruptly that poor Skylar stumbled into me.

"This is getting tiresome," she muttered, walking past me. "I'll be waiting in the car. Don't bother, Kaitlynn. Some things never change. Once a dog, always a dog."

Her long blonde hair swayed around her shoulders as she stormed out of the house.

I couldn't bring myself to turn. It felt like if I so much as glanced at him, I'd fall apart. It was a familiar pattern. Time and time again, he played the victim, and time and time again, I fell for it. The first instance seemed insignificant compared to what had just happened. At first, it merely consisted of a quick gaze across the room or a peek over the edge of his red plastic beer cup. It was easy to brush off. Everyone did it, right? I mean, I even found myself checking out some of the fraternity brothers, but that happened before I really got to know them, mind you. Then those glances lingered, growing longer from five or ten seconds to minutes. How I failed to notice that he acted like an animal hunting its prey could only be blamed on denial. To make matters worse, he didn't feel content until he had conquered it. Until he had tasted the forbidden fruit. Except, in this case, the fruit were young women, some of whom were my friends. Well, "friends" might be a stretch. The majority of them were acquaintances. Nonetheless, it was awful. And then it became a friend. A good friend. Scratch that, a great friend. That night, I found out the true reality of my situation. That was when I started paying attention. But by that point, I was too far gone. Too in love with Ash to see the truth. He stayed with me, right? He loved them and left them, and we remained intact, or so I thought. I foolishly blamed the other women. After all, he was taken. How dare they mess around with someone else's boyfriend. When reality hit me like a ton of bricks, it nearly destroyed me. Olivia proved to be the breaking point. She had never been to a party at the Alpha Pi house before. Always buried in her studies, she rarely came out of hiding. But that night, six months ago, she did. Skylar and I were thrilled. We spent hours doing her makeup, and when we were finished, she looked absolutely stunning. The party was intended to be a fun break after a week of hard studying and worrying about our futures, and it ended in disaster.

"Kaitlynn..." his voice was soft and pleading. "Won't you look at me? Am I so repulsive to you now?"

I went rigid. He was doing it again. Playing the victim like the last time.

The memory of that night six months ago flooded back into my mind. Skylar and I had been separated from Olivia the moment we stepped foot into the Alpha Pi house. It was a popular party destination, and that night was no exception. Amidst the rush of the crowd and the blaring music, we found ourselves engulfed in a chaotic atmosphere, and separated. Later, we stumbled upon Olivia, flushed and unsteady, near the kitchen door.

"He wouldn't leave me alone until I drank," she had confessed, her words heavy with distress. Her once pristine sapphire blue dress was now stained with beer. "I just wanted it to be over with, so I gave in, and then he..." her lower lip trembled with anguish, "he pushed me against the wall and he... Oh Kaitlynn, I'm sorry."

I'll never forget her glistening eyes. The doe-eyed brainiac turned vixen had been assaulted. By Ash. My boyfriend.

I balled my fists so hard my palms stung from the nails digging into my flesh at the memory. Months later, we found ourselves in a similar situation with Ashton playing the victim.

"Kaitlynn, please."

He brushed it off that night, despite hours of shouting in his room. He fooled me, preying on my vulnerabilities, expressing his love, begging me not to go, wondering if he could ever make things right. I eventually caved, but I've never been able to forgive myself for what happened that night. I've always blamed myself for burying the memory, which only hurt Olivia more. This day was different.

I turned around slowly, and Ashton's expression matched my expectations. The concern, the pleading, the sadness—it was all there, as if on instant recall. How many times had he pulled this act with other women? How many times had they fallen for it? Or was I the only one?

When Ashton rushed toward me I jerked my hand up, halting him in his tracks. Tears welled up in my eyes as I fought to control my emotions. "No. Ash, I've endured your wandering gaze, your flirting, and I've even ignored your affairs, but this..." Tears streamed down my cheeks, and I let them. "No more. We're done, Ash. Don't call me."

Blinded by tears, I spun around and hurried towards the door. Flying down the porch steps, the only thing I heard was the loud smack of the screen door closing behind me. Ashton and I were over, and somehow, I'd get through it.

CHAPTER 18

*S*kylar and I drove in silence, raindrops pelting the car. I'd given her the keys since my vision was blurry through my tears. Fortunately, she didn't push. We never did. When one of us was ready to talk, we would. It was the unspeakable rule between us, and it had worked since we'd met at Freshman orientation. That was a little over a year ago. Gosh, had it really been that long?

We pulled into the parking lot of my apartment, and Sky turned to me at the exact moment my phone *beeped*.

Her gaze shifted towards the phone resting on my lap. "How many times will you let it beep before silencing the darn thing?"

Skylar reached over and grasped my cold hands in hers, her green eyes filled with concern. "Listen, why don't you silence it for now while we figure out where to find Bradley? We'll ask him some questions and then regroup. How does that sound?"

The phone chimed again. Another message from Ashton. In the brief journey, he'd sent at least twenty, each one pleading for forgiveness, vowing to change his ways. The latest one proposed a weekend trip to Paris. Silencing the phone, I bowed my head, cradling it in my hands while Skylar rubbed my back. A nagging pulse between my temples surged, and I desperately needed some migraine medication.

"I know where Bradley is," I croaked, my voice raw. I sat up and wiped my sleeve against my puffy, sore eyes.

"Really? Where?" Skylar put the car in reverse, ready to go, but I laid a hand on hers.

"Wait. First, let me get some medication. My head's exploding."

Skylar pulled into the spot again, and shut the engine off with a clunk. She jogged around the rear of the car and opened my door while I dragged myself out and trudged up the steps to my apartment.

"I need a dog." It looked the same as I'd left it this morning, but something was missing. Since encountering the unforeseeable, a glaring void had consumed my life, casting a vast shadow over everything.

Skylar huffed, her hands on her slender hips. "Honey, a dog isn't the solution."

In my quest to find relief, I accidentally knocked over several bottles in the kitchen cabinet, but eventually found the migraine medicine and swallowed two. I then plodded across the open floor plan of my apartment and plopped onto the bed, hugging a decorative pillow to my chest. When I moved in, my father stuck glow-in-the-dark stars on the ceiling for the insomnia I'd suffered since the age of five. At that time in life, my mom had my IQ tested, and her incessant study sessions afterward drove me to extreme anxiety. Apparently, I was to become the next neurosurgeon. Once Brenda Dahl made up her mind about something, nothing and no one kept her from it, and that extended to my education. My dad had hung the stars as a kind of peace offering, and I remember him saying to imagine floating among them. I would squeeze my eyes shut and summon the twinkling lights suspended around me. Soon, I'd found myself happily alone, soaring amidst them, envisioning distant lands, and within an hour, they would lull me to sleep. Regrettably, however, the morning light would inevitably filter through my window blinds and my mother's torment would resume.

I sat on the bed and diverted my gaze away from the ceiling. When Skylar stifled a yawn, I observed dark circles under her voluminous black lashes. She squeezed my ankle, her face bearing signs of exhaustion.

I tensed. "Are you okay?" I asked, pulling myself upright, folding my legs underneath me.

Skylar shrugged. "Morgana."

"Ah." *That* name conveyed volumes, and in an instant, I found myself scrambling on all fours to embrace her.

"I'm fine."

I kept my arm draped around her shoulders while our legs dangled off the end of the bed. Hers were like a movie star's, long and sensual, while mine were lean and athletic. While we were complete opposites that way, we were of kindred mindsets.

"Is there anything I can do?" I knew well the frustrations of intrusive family members, particularly my own mother. In Skylar's case, her grandmother surpassed them all. I shuddered at the thought of the tales she'd shared with Olivia and me about her punishments in that cellar room.

Skylar offered a faint smile. "She's confiscated Aunt Hazel's cell."

"What?" I gasped. "How?"

"Hazel's in the hospital. She's fine," she hurriedly reassured, noticing my immediate distress. "But Morgana intercepted the call when I called her. I have no means of contacting her now, and I refuse to involve my sister."

"Will she be okay?"

"I hope so."

A shadow of doubt marred her features, belying the truth she tried shielding from those close to her. After Skylar's mom died, her Great Aunt Hazel became her caretaker, even though the courts granted her maternal grandmother, Morgana, custody. From what I'd gathered, Morgana lacked the mothering instinct and was more into controlling Skylar than anything else.

"We need a distraction." I slid off the bed and planted my hands on my hips.

"Oh, no." She shook her head. "I'm not a fan of your distractions."

"I'm *offended*, my dear Sky."

We burst into fits of laughter until our sides ached. It felt refreshing to laugh again. I had almost forgotten how that felt.

"You know the drill," I remarked, making my way toward the bathroom.

Despite Sky's groan, she got off the bed and followed me. Once we made it to my walk-in closet, we searched my rack of dresses. Due to her roommate's excessive obsession with cleanliness, she'd decided to store the majority of her clothes at my place for the last six months. Since I frequently stayed with Ash, it was logical for her to stay at my place.

The hooks screeched against the metal pole as we sifted through dress after dress, a sign of our bountiful excursions to the co-op store over the past year. The rack sagged in the middle to the point I feared it would break. Maybe it was time to take some of them. Besides, we'd only worn three dresses apiece out of the thirty plus hung on the rack.

Skylar pulled a bright red slip dress off the shelf and hung it close to her, checking her reflection in my long closet mirror hung on the back of the door. Her lips pulled into a pout. "Ugh. I hate red." She rehung the dress and searched again.

"It's not the color you hate," I knowingly smiled at her. "Sky, everything looks good on you. Heck, you could even look great in a trash bag."

Skylar's usual lightheartedness failed to surface. She whipped through another three dresses, roughly shoving them aside.

"Hey, if you want to wear it, just wear it. It's all in your head. Red looks marvelous on you."

If I could throttle that last boyfriend of hers I would, but seeing as how I'd end up in jail right beside Krissy, I'd better focus on the task at hand.

"I picked out a peacock green and blue slip dress, our favorite type, and held it out for Skylar's approval. When she barely glanced at it, I stepped so close it forced her to look at it.

"That's your favorite," she said.

"I insist. It always looked better on you anyway. I'm sure I'll find something else. Take it."

Initially she declined, opting instead to flip through three additional dresses with a derisive snort before returning to me still clutching the original dress.

"Alright, fine, but you should wear this one."

Skylar reached behind me and pulled out a pale blue shift dress. The see-through outer shell had circular designs in another shade of blue, resulting in a breathtaking effect.

"Sky, that's *your* favorite."

She grinned with a mischievous twinkle in her eye, her sense of humor restored. "It suits you better. Take it. I insist."

Skylar looked at me with anticipation. "Alright, we've got the dresses. What's the plan? Where are we going and what mischief are you plotting?"

"First we dress and get all dolled up." I stepped aside, facing the mirror, holding the pale blue creation against my body. "Then we strike."

CHAPTER 19

Skylar tugged at the thigh-high hemline as yet another young man whistled loudly through his teeth. Three men with backpacks stood outside the college library steps salivating after us.

"I still don't understand why we had to dress up for this." Skylar's body had grown a bit since the last time we'd tried on the outfits. She'd become more curvy, which brought the hemline a little too close to her birthday suit. Too close for her liking. From my vantage point, however, it was exactly what we needed. As much as I hated to admit it, the feminine form was a tool to wield, though only as a last resort. With Krissy in jail charged for a crime she didn't commit, this was that time.

We skittered up the steps with the young men drooling, Skylar tugging in vain to keep her rounded backside from showing too much upper thigh.

We went inside the building, and I made an immediate right turn.

"Hey," she said, struggling to keep up. "Why are we here, or is that a secret too?"

We walked down the musty 1960s-era library stacks and rounded a corner where the slated stairs led to the second floor. Our heels clacked on each one, drawing a few perturbed eyes our way. Once on the landing, I made a beeline toward the opposite side of the rectangular building, passing by nooks filled with students buried in their studies, sneaking bites of forbidden snacks or a sip of water. We walked on the worn lime green carpet, littered with decades-old gum that had been carelessly discarded. All the while, Skylar kept whispering questions which I left unanswered. She'd understand soon enough.

The section of stacks opened up to an area the size of a 10x10 foot room where three study tables and chairs stood alongside a copy machine. Sitting at the center table was the bright-eyed man we'd come to see. Nose deep in a book, he lunched on a cheese sandwich. He apparently wasn't worried about the librarian overlords ready to kick anyone out for breaking the rules.

When we reached the end of the table he looked up with a blank expression. It was like he was in a different world solving complex mathematical equations or world hunger. His forehead crinkled. "May I help you?"

I pulled out a chair. "May we sit?"

He nodded, and soon we were face to face with him.

His criminal justice book was cracked open to a chapter on police brutality, and the freshly highlighted text leapt from the page. He stared intently, and it only took a mere two seconds to become completely focused on Sky.

I fought the urge to grin.

"Bradley, what's your take on Krissy?" I asked.

Bradley capped his highlighter with a click and dropped it on his open book. "We've already discussed this."

"Not entirely." I leaned my elbows on the table. "What haven't you told me?"

Bradley flipped two notebooks closed, tucking them into his backpack lying on the tabletop, though not before I caught they both had the Harvard Law design on them.

"What's to tell?" He closed the bag with a zip and rose to leave.

I gave him a stern look. His face stiffened, every muscle tense.

"For starters," I said, undeterred by his change in demeanor, "explain those pictures."

Confusion clouded his expression. "Which ones? You'll need to be more specific."

"Trent handed you some pictures before he died. What were they of?"

Bradley slung the backpack over his shoulder. "That's personal." He backed away from his chair.

"I'm certain the police will be interested."

He had taken a few steps when he stopped abruptly.

Skylar glanced at me, a gleam in her eye. Maybe we were onto something.

Bradley scratched the back of his head, but instead of addressing me, his attention shifted to Skylar. She met his gaze evenly. His demeanor softened as he looked at her. Approaching her, he grinned.

"Your friend sure does ask a lot of questions, but not you," he remarked, his eyes studying Skylar's face. "Why is that?"

"I'm not the brains behind this operation."

"No," he said, adjusting the sliding backpack on his shoulder. "Why are you two friends? It doesn't make sense. You're the beauty," he glanced at me then back to Skylar, "and she's the brains. It doesn't add up."

Skylar's confusion advanced to irritation. "Well, Mr. Harvard," she crossed her arms against her chest, "not everything is as black and white as you make it. Women are as diverse as anything on this planet. It's not a one-size-fits-all kind of world. I admire Kaitlynn's inquisitiveness, her intellect, and her beauty. It's a shame not everyone can see it."

"It seems I've been mistaken about you." He inched closer, and she visibly tensed. "Don't sell yourself short, Sky. You're not as dumb as others might think. As for Kaitlynn," he cast a cold stare at me, "tell the police about them if you must, but it can only bring pain. It won't free Krissy. She's got her own reasons for being behind bars."

"Such as?" I pushed.

"Krissy thought she could control Trent. Nobody got one over on Trent."

"Blackmail? Krissy had something on him? What?" Krissy was too upset to tell Connor, and I mistakenly believed Trent had a compromising picture of her, but perhaps not.

"Does it matter? He's dead."

"It might help free her from jail, yes. What did Krissy have over Trent, Bradley? Either tell us or tell the police. I really don't care."

I was tired of all these games. The Alpha Pi fraternity house was brimming with them. Scratch that. The house was infested with deceit, dishonesty, and betrayal. How did I not pick up on this stuff earlier? Was I so smitten with Ash that I deluded myself into turning a blind eye not only to his skirting ways but more heinous behavior too? The thought left me queasy.

I pulled out my cell and dialed the local police department.

"Stop." I hung up after I heard, *"Detective Shaw, can I help you?"* on the other end.

Bradley's gaze shifted to Skylar. "Krissy had an untoward photo of Trent, and it was with a faculty member. The professor made me promise not to tell anyone for fear of losing her job, and honestly, she's probably too good for this university, anyway."

"Professor Fletcher." No sooner had I said that than I was up on my feet.

Bradley called out, "Wait." He placed a hand on Skylar's forearm. "There's something else." He swallowed hard. "Connor sent you, didn't he?"

Skylar and I stared at him, unblinking.

"Listen, Connor's not as innocent as he's making himself out to be."

"Meaning?" I asked.

"Let's just say that there's more than one frat brother with a straying eye."

We'd seen it Connor's lust toward the professor. Was the interest returned? There was no way of knowing from the photo, since she'd been smiling directly at the camera. However, something else struck me about Bradley.

"Were you in on the tattooing? Did you participate in drugging the women, putting them in uncompromising positions, and taking photos of them? Did you rate them too?"

Bradley's guarded expression unwaveringly held mine. "To an extent. Yes, I rated women. It was a part of hazing, but no, I wasn't a part of any drugging or tattooing. I tried reporting it to Professor Fletcher, and look where that got her."

I threw out a hand for support on the table as my knees buckled. Professor Fletcher had been out for revenge. The whole thing was revolting and ran so much deeper under the surface than I'd realized. From Skylar's disgusted expression, she agreed.

"What did he have on you, Bradley?" I asked. "If you didn't participate in the roofies, the tattooing, and you turned him in, then what *did* Trent have on you?"

Bradley looked down to the floor. "I've been stealing tests from certain professors. When exam time comes around, people pay me for them. I'm not proud of it." He then met my shocked gaze. "Please believe me. I never would have done it if there'd been any other way to get into Harvard Law. I've applied time and time again for under-grad, and they turned me down each time. I needed great grades, and that's what I've done. No one will stand in the way of that. I've worked too hard."

I stiffened. "No one?"

The implication hit him deeply and he backed away. "Not that. I would never..." Neither Skylar nor I required further explanation. "If you decide to report me, I'll understand," he said, bowing his head. "But please, give me a heads-up. I know I don't deserve it."

I stared for a moment longer. His slouched posture, bowed head, and hand stuffed in his pockets showed a defeated man. Was it right to cheat for admittance? No. Was it understandable? Maybe. From the many conversations I'd had with Ashton, he'd mentioned Bradley's meager upbringing. Bradley had worked hard to mask it with his fancy clothing, shoes, and backpack, but if you looked closer, they were knockoff brands. From the surface, he appeared, as he claimed, to come from a family of means. Only his closest friends knew otherwise.

"Fine," I said against my better judgement.

"Kaitlynn!" Skylar gasped. "We should turn him in right now."

Bradley held out his wrists to Skylar. "You're right, blondie. Turn me in. I deserve it."

I sighed. "Enough with the dramatics. I'll call the police shortly, but first, tell me more about Connor."

Bradley dropped his hands by his sides. "What do you want to know?"

CHAPTER 20

$\mathcal{T}$he orange and brown leaves kicked up into a stir at our feet as Skylar and I stalked down the outside library steps. We turned to our right and headed for the math and science building. Neither of us spoke until we entered the upstairs room. The desk was littered with stacks of ungraded papers, and a posterboard displaying a complex math problem sat to the right of the cramped desk. Above the desk, the Math-a-thon Champions banner was tacked to the wall.

"Hello, girls." Professor Fletcher slammed her phone down and smiled at us. "What can I do for you?"

"Why didn't you tell us you were sleeping with Connor and Trent?" I blurted.

Professor Fletcher's face grew taught. "Close the door."

Skylar treaded over to do so while I planted my palms on the teacher's desk. "You lied to me."

The door shut with a click.

"I think of it as an exclusion," Professor Fletcher said, shuffling ungraded tests and showing no signs of duress.

"Exclusion?" I snorted. "Sleeping with one student is bad enough. But two?"

She leaned into her chair and studied me through designer glasses. "What have you really come here for?"

"Did you have anything to do with Trent's death?"

"No."

"Could either Warren or Connor have killed him?"

Her eyes narrowed. "I can't say for certain."

"Why not?"

The professor removed her glasses and tossed them onto the desk. "Connor is a good person and—"

"A good person?" Skylar scoffed. "So it's fine to sleep with them, right?"

Professor Fletcher bristled. "Trent was an adult, over the age of 18. Heck, he was over 21, not underage, and I... I loved him," she said.

Skylar closed her mouth, visibly struggling to contain her anger.

"Loved?" I focused intently on the professor. "In the past tense?"

A crack formed in her otherwise stern gaze. "Connor wants what I can't give."

"Which is?" I asked, undeterred.

"A relationship. My work comes first. It always has. Trent and Connor, they were looking for a good time or an escape. What I didn't expect was for Trent to drug me and video me doing things I'd never do sober, and Connor..." She looked down at her intertwined hands rested on her desktop. "Connor needs to move on."

"He's already got a girlfriend," Skylar offered from behind me, her voice flat with judgement.

Professor Fletcher perked up. "That's... that's great."

"No." I shook my head. "He's had this girlfriend for two years. Way before you showed up. And that girlfriend is in jail for Trent's murder."

Her gaze held mine. "I had no idea."

"Is that a lie?" I asked. "You seem pretty good at it."

She smiled. "I deserve that, but no. It's not." She abruptly rose from her seat, leaning forward to grab something off her desk. As she did so, her blouse dipped, revealing a tiny gray-tailed dragon tattooed on her cleavage.

"Here." She offered me a folded letter. "It's my resignation. I'd planned on mailing it, but it seems better to deliver it in person. Today. From this point forward, I'm no longer a professor here. Tomorrow, I'll pack and leave."

"But the murder," Skylar blurted. "You can't leave. What if—"

"I murdered Trent?" Professor Fletcher shook her head. "I didn't. To ease your minds, I've already told the police everything, and I've given them my forwarding address."

Skylar and I gaped at the professor.

I snatched the note from her and read. Sure enough, it was a full confession. No doubt this would end her career.

"What will you do now?" I asked, now feeling awkward and intrusive. I laid the letter on top of some papers.

"I don't know, and I don't care." She breathed in deeply. "It's a new day, right? Maybe I'll jet-set around the globe, or start a non-profit school for underprivileged girls somewhere." She opened her leather briefcase, tossed in her phone, and gripped the handle. "Or maybe I'll start a non-profit for women against sexism in the workplace." A small grin emerged as she put on her tortoise-colored sunglasses. "Either way, I'll get my justice or die trying."

Her heels clicked on the tiled flooring as she stepped around her desk and went for the door. Swinging it wide open, she faced us. "Keep up the good fight, ladies. The world needs more brains and brawn like you, and thank you."

"For what?" I asked in surprise.

"For freeing me. I feel lighter than I have in ages, and I can rest peacefully knowing you two are on the case. Remember," she walked into the hallway, her heels clacking along the way, "burn those photos. Goodbye, and good luck."

With a flick of her wrist in farewell, she walked to the end of the hall and vanished from our sight.

Skylar stared down the hallway after her. "That was unexpected."

"Yeah," I agreed. "Didn't see that one coming. I wish her well."

Skylar hooked her arm through mine. "What do you say we take our brains and brawn and regroup at the Shake Shack?"

"Deal. Except I'm paying this time. Mom's sent a peace offering, which means it'll be an extra-large shake for me."

Skylar groaned. "What's she done this time?"

I shrugged. "Not even the faintest idea, but it must be a doozy because she sent a whopping two hundred dollars."

Skylar squealed with glee. "Shopping time!"

"After the shakes."

Skylar's quietness drew my attention. "What's wrong?"

"Nothing. I get a sense things are only revving up. Like we're in danger." She shook her head. "No matter. It's probably nothing. I watched that horror movie you told me about."

"I warned you *not* to watch that, remember?"

"Yeah, but then I got to thinking."

I grimaced. "I've got to keep my mouth shut. I bet you didn't sleep at all."

"Not a wink, but that's not what's bogged me down."

I glanced at her slender profile. Her beautiful blonde hair sat in waves around her head and shoulders, and she'd put only the necessary foundation, blush, and lip gloss on, and she was still somehow runway ready.

"What's bogging you down?"

We exited the building arm-in-arm and set off for the car. The wind had picked up, and a chill cut through my shirt, making me shiver. I hugged more tightly to Skylar's arm as we picked up the pace.

"What's after the shake and shopping?"

We walked in silence for another couple of minutes before something popped to mind. "We need to see a jailbird."

Skylar's forehead crunched.

"First," I said, grinning, "let's stuff our bellies."

"Then we make the jailbird sing?" Skylar's shoulders relaxed and put a bounce back in her step as we approached the car.

We zoomed out of the lot and were at the Shake Shack five minutes later, but my mind kept replaying Sky's last words. *The jailbird singing.* Would she? Or was she guilty, after all?

CHAPTER 21

*T*he Shake Shack buzzed with activity. We ordered and snagged the first empty table we found.

"Remind me again why you think Krissy may have..." Skylar scooted her chair closer to the table and leaned forward, her voice low, "...killed Trent?"

The chair beside mine slammed into my thigh.

"Sorry." A female dressed in a naughty nurse's outfit giggled in passing. A guy dressed as a superhero chased her off with his playful swats.

I rubbed my sore thigh and then noticed the entire restaurant was brimming with costumed college students in various costumes.

"Is it Halloween already?"

Skylar slapped her palm on the table. "Focus, Kaitlynn."

"Right. Um, if Connor, Warren, and Professor Fletcher were all telling the truth—"

"Which is debatable," Skylar interrupted with an arch of her brow.

"That leaves Krissy. To be honest, she *does* have plenty of motive. What if Trent threatened to sick his dad on her? Sounds like the man is feared."

Skylar puffed out her cheeks. "You've really got to dig your nose out of those books and away from Ash once in a while. Trent's father is a high-powered attorney in the news almost every month. His celebrity clients are the worst, and they practically get away with murder. If Krissy had anything substantial over Trent, I doubt he'd wait to tell his father. The photo of Professor Fletcher couldn't have been the smoking gun."

"Yes, but think about it, Sky. What if it was something so horrible he wanted to keep it from his father?"

Skylar pursed her lips. "That would have to be something pretty terrible, Katydid. I don't know."

"Don't know what?"

I tensed, unable to twist my neck and look up. Skylar's immediate eye roll only set my nerves on edge.

Her chair legs screeched on the floor as she stood. "I'm checking on our food."

She shot me a pointed glance before spinning around and storming past the counter, weaving through a group of people dressed as cheerleaders and football players, and then making a right turn toward the door.

The door closed behind her, my view gradually obscured.

"Kaitlynn, I've messaged at least a dozen times. Can't we talk?"

I stared up at Ashton, who scrutinized my face for any telltale sign of forgiveness or weakness. Among the few in the restaurant without a costume, he was wearing khakis and a long-sleeved maroon polo shirt, which brought out the golden flecks in his irises. From his deep voice that rumbled in his chest, to his soft lips, he'd been my whole world. Everything rose and set with him. No longer. At this moment, the only thing I saw was a typical guy looking to score and keep up appearances with his parents, his friends, and practically anyone else by dating me. Although introspection was a slippery slope I rarely traveled, these last two days had forced me down it, and what I saw left me wanting to break free and run. From my squeaky clean academic record, my average looks, and my introverted ways, I'd always wondered what drew Ashton to me. Sure, Skylar and Olivia warned me, but I'd turned a blind eye to those boyish grins, flattering words, and caresses. Hook, line, and sinker, I'd believed him. Looking back, however, once he'd gotten me, the flirtations with other females had started. Heck, he didn't waste any time hooking up with other women.

Ashton's eyes were drawn to a vampire sashaying past, his gaze fixated on her ample rear.

"You're unbelievable," I snapped.

"What?" He looked completely shocked.

"Really?" I huffed. "I saw you looking at her butt. Don't deny it, Ash."

I forcibly rose and the chair tumbled to the floor with a crash.

"Wait." Ash seized my wrist, preventing me from leaving. "Hear me out."

I stared straight ahead at the two couples by the front door. Both females sat on their dates' laps, their arms wrapped around their necks. They all laughed at some unheard joke, and my heart plummeted to my toes.

"Please?" Ashton implored, sensing my reluctance to move or respond.

I could hear the desperation in his voice, the pain. But for the first time, I remained indifferent. I turned my head toward him, struggling to contain the anger swelling within me. With fists clenched tightly, I etched into my memory every contour of his face, fueled by a mixture of frustration and determination.

"No, Ash. You may have been my dream once, but I see you for the pathetic excuse of a man you really are. Now let me go." I wrenched my wrist away with a tug.

Shoulders back, I walked forward. Without looking back, I grabbed my order at the counter and stormed out, hearing the remnants of laughter broken by the slam of the restaurant door.

Skylar waited in the passenger seat of my car, buckled and cross.

"What took you so long?" she barked, but I caught the glimmer of happiness she couldn't hide.

"Cut the act, Sky. I'm sure you saw everything."

She abandoned her angry façade, pivoting in her seat with a spark of delight in her eyes as she grabbed the bags. Picking out her cheese-burger, she bit into it and mumbled, "Tell me what I couldn't hear. All of it."

She stopped for a sip of her peanut butter fudge shake and then nodded for me to continue.

I relayed the short conversation.

Skylar swallowed and let out a low whistle. "About bleeping time, girlie. High five."

Her good mood was infectious, and soon we were driving down the road, pulling into the police station lot in no time flat. The smell of grease and onions filled the car as we both chomped on our burgers and stared at the front door.

Skylar chewed her straw. "You think they will they let you visit her?"

I shook my head. "I don't have the faintest idea, but we won't find out sitting here."

We put the burger wrappers in the bag and stepped out of the car. The journey to the police station door felt like an eternity. When we walked in, a mix of body odor and stale coffee hit us full blast the second the door shut.

After wiping my sweaty palms on my hips, Skylar and I walked up to the uniformed cop at the desk without hesitation.

"We're here to see Krissy," I stated, the squeak in my voice betraying my attempts to sound assertive. There was something about being around cops that made my neck hairs stand on end. It felt as though I was already on trial, guilty of a crime I hadn't committed.

The officer's bold grey eyes held mine and he declared, "We are not in the habit of allowing visitors access to anyone unless accompanied by an attorney. In this case, I would also need a last name."

The twinkle in his eyes softened his stern features, exposing slight wrinkles around his otherwise smooth-shaven face. In his late thirties, if I were to hazard a guess, he had the typical persona of a cop, except for the dad pooch.

"Right," I mumbled. What now? "Ah, we've been sent by Krissy's attorney."

"Is that so?" The cop's lips quirked into a faint smile.

"Yes, her attorney said we could talk with her. Only for a few minutes."

"And that attorney's name would be?" He eyed both Skylar and me in turn.

"Uh, I... it's..." Skylar began and fizzled out. "Look," she laid a hand on the counter, "we're friends of hers. Krissy's a lot of things but—"

The cop arched a brow.

"I mean, she's *not* a murderer. I didn't mean..."

"What she's trying to say," I stepped in, seeing the futility of it evident on the amused cop's face, "is that Krissy is frightened, and we're here to talk. That's it. There isn't any way for us to see her? If only for a few minutes?"

The officer stared at me, mulling over what we'd said while both Sky and I fidgeted under his intense gaze. He leaned over the desk, his voice low. "You have five minutes. Any longer, and I'll lock you in there with her."

Skylar and I exchanged a high-five. Our excitement quickly faded when he rolled his eyes, muttering, "I need to stop being such a sucker."

Down a long corridor, past an open room full of desks with ringing phones and cops inputting information from a few hand-cuffed folks, we turned left where he opened a door to a 10x10 room. On the right wall was a two-way mirror, and in the center was a metal table with two chairs on either side.

"Sit. I'll bring Krissy in shortly."

His keys clanged on his hip as he left, leaving the door slightly ajar.

"Hey," Skylar whispered, sneaking a glance at the mirror. "What now? We're knee deep in suspects. If she asks about an update—"

"She will." I kept my voice low and fixated on the open door.

"Then what?" Skylar hissed.

We were cut off when Krissy shuffled into the room. Her mascara had streaked down her cheeks, belying hours of crying into the night and day. The orange jumper she wore stood in stark contrast to her pale cheeks and disheveled hair.

"Kaitlynn?" Her voice quivered as she rushed forward.

"No touching," barked the officer. "Five minutes. Starting now."

The cop left, shutting the door behind him. Krissy shuffled around the table and took a seat. Elbows on the table, she leaned forward. "Have you found him? When am I getting out of here? This place is creepy and I want my dad. Why hasn't he come? Didn't you call him?"

She searched our faces expectantly.

"Wait," Skylar said, "you haven't seen your father?"

Krissy gave a faint shake of the head. Tears welled up. "I haven't seen an attorney yet either." She balled her fists. Her mouth flattened into a straight line.

"What about your call?" I asked. "You're allowed a phone call."

Krissy swiped at the tears falling down her face. "Dad's not answering." She squeezed her eyes shut as we watched the pain consume her. "He's probably on his yacht in the Bahamas with his latest conquest. They won't let me call anyone else."

Incredible. His daughter was behind bars under suspicion of murder, and he was out enjoying himself with a woman who, judging by the sound of it, couldn't have been much older than Krissy.

I moved to comfort her, then hesitated, recalling the officer's stern warning. "Right. Listen, Krissy, we haven't got a lot of time. We need to ask you some questions."

"Anything." She rubbed her palms together, her eyes wild. "I'll answer anything."

"Connor mentioned Trent's attempted assault."

Krissy's sole sign of emotion was a brief narrowing of her eyes. "Go on."

"We know about the roofies," Skylar added.

Krissy snorted. "He was a right louse. Whatever Trent wanted, Trent got. No wasn't an answer for him. He saw it as a game."

"Of cat and mouse," I said.

She nodded.

"What do you know about Bradley and the cheating?"

"The tests?" she asked. "He's been doing that for a while. Heck, I've even bought some off of him. Not proud to say that, and I'll probably get expelled for it, but that's the least of my worries."

"What about Connor?"

She frowned. "What about him?"

I stole a glance at Skylar, but she had that distant expression, which meant I was driving solo on this one. There was no real way to say this, so I might as well spit it out. "Were you aware he was sleeping with a professor?"

Krissy's eyes widened in surprise. "What? That's not possible." She shook her head. "Connor loves me. He…" She looked from her tightly balled hands to me.

"Krissy, the perfume…"

She shook her head more violently, tears threatening to make their return. "No," she croaked.

"She knew," Skylar said pointedly.

"Back with us." I grinned over at my dear friend. To Krissy I said, "How long had it been going on?"

Krissy slumped in the chair, defeated. "A few months. Maybe more."

"Did you confront the professor?"

"Fletcher?" She uttered her name with disdain. "You bet I did. I even threatened to tell the administration."

"Why didn't you?" Skylar asked.

Krissy sighed. "If I did, he'd never forgive me." After all the hurt, she still held out hope for their relationship.

"Were you aware of Trent drugging Professor Fletcher?"

The surprise transformed into a smirk. "Good."

Skylar and I jerked in surprise. "Good?" I repeated.

The smirk faded as quickly as it came. "I'm sorry." She rubbed a fist across her forehead. "That was insensitive."

A rap on the door made us all jump. Fear flashed across Krissy's face. "Please help me. There're women back there that keep hitting me. You've got to get me out of here."

"Krissy, what did you hold over Trent?"

Her face twisted in confusion. "Pardon?"

"Bradley said—"

"Bradley," she snapped. "He's one to talk. Have Bradley talk about Big Bear." She snorted. "For that matter, have a talk with Ashton. It would be... enlightening."

The door swung open. "Alright, ladies. Time's up."

Krissy stood and shuffled toward the door. "Trent's done worse before, Kaitlynn," she said before she stepped out. "He's taken something forcibly. Corner Bradley. He'll be the one to cave. Him, or Ashton, if you're still talking."

"Come on," the cop snapped, tugging her arm with a firm grip.

"Ashton's hiding a secret, Kaitlynn. Cozy up to him, and he may just spill it."

And like that, she was gone.

"What's that supposed to mean?" Skylar asked, staring after her.

"I have no idea. Come on."

I hopped up and jogged down the hallway with Skylar on my heels.

"Where to?"

"I think I know a way to figure all this out. First, let's get back to the apartment and look over those photos again. There's something we're missing."

"And second?"

We stepped out into the brisk autumn air. The chill sent shivers down my spine.

"I call Ash."

Skylar groaned. "He's not worth it, Katydid."

"No," I sighed as we made our way to the car. "You've got it all wrong."

"

We were soon flying down the streets toward home. I pulled into the apartment parking lot.

"Are you getting back together with him?" Skylar asked.

"No, definitely not." I rested my hands on my thighs and turned to Skylar.

Her confusion melted away, replaced by understanding. "You're luring him, aren't you? It's a trap. Are you sure you can do this?"

"No, I'm not sure, but it's the only way."

I pulled out my cell and typed in a message, then we headed up the steps to my second-story flat. We entered the apartment and within two steps, my phone buzzed. Looking down, my heart leapt in my chest.

"He took the bait." I smirked up at Skylar. "Who's ready for another makeover?"

CHAPTER 22

"Kaitlynn." Ashton abruptly stood, rattling the plates and utensils. He hustled around to pull out my chair.

I stiffly sat and placed the cloth napkin in my lap, not making eye contact.

When he was seated again, Ashton offered the bread basket. I waved it off.

The enticing aroma of spaghetti sauce, sweet and spicy with a generous amount of garlic, filled the air. Despite my reservations, my stomach growled. Italian cuisine had always been a favorite of mine, but I hadn't come here for the food or for reconciliation.

"Thank you for coming," Ashton said. He glanced around the empty 1980s styled restaurant. The red and white checkered plastic tablecloths and the lit squat red candle holders on each table created a time warp. The brown paneling on the walls added to the darkened ambience. And while most people probably would have turned their noses up at it, I loved this place. Ash had taken me to it on our first date. Afterward, we'd strolled around Lakeland Lake listening to the crickets and other insects buzzing by. The memory made me squirm in my seat and fidget with my utensils.

Remember what you're here for, I reminded myself.

I fixed on his hopeful stare and plastered on a bright smile. "I figured we needed to clear the air." I broke off a piece of the bread, giving into my stomach and nerves, and dipped it into the olive oil beside it, then popping it into my mouth.

Concern reflected in his eyes, taking the place of the hope that had been present seconds earlier. "Right. Listen, I'm sorry about all of it. I shouldn't have involved you in any of this."

It was my turn for confusion. The crusty exterior of the bread lodged in my throat and I reached for the water while he rushed on like a steam train barreling downhill.

"Let me set the record straight. I didn't mean to fall for you. Honest. But after all the time we spent together, I succumbed to your wit and smarts, but besides all that, you're absolutely beautiful, Kaitlynn."

I gulped the water to dislodge the bread wreaking havoc in my throat. Taking my silence as a positive sign, he rushed on.

"Vic and I—"

"Vic?" I spluttered, feeling the heat rise in my face and neck.

He failed to notice my distress. Plowing ahead, he said, "We were high school sweethearts. When she followed me to college, it seemed inevitable that we'd get married. After having met you, um, well, let's say that I'm not so sure anymore. You're amazing, and if it weren't for this whole thing with Trent, I may never have found out."

Ashton reached across the table and took my hand, rubbing his thumb up and down the side of it, while I reeled from what he'd sprung on me.

"Vic's upset," he said, "and I understand. Heck, you're angry, and that's understandable too, but hear me out."

I sat there utterly speechless. My mind raced, trying to make sense of what he'd said, but I couldn't seem to connect the dots.

"Trent was a real jerk. When we initially started this, you were not a part of the plan. It wasn't until Trent showed an interest that we had to include you, but not as his next conquest. Vic had compelled me to protect you, and please trust me when I say that we never meant to hurt you."

"You... Vic..." I pulled my sweaty hand from his, sitting ramrod straight in the chair. My neck hurt from the tension. Even though I wanted nothing more than to look elsewhere, I couldn't turn away. "What are you saying? Why are you telling me this now?"

The waiter arrived with our meals, silencing him.

The scent of garlic wafted up, and I clamped a hand over my churning tummy. While I struggled to breathe, I gaped at the steaming meatballs and spaghetti and waited for the waiter to leave.

Ashton pushed his plate aside. "Warren messaged, saying you were asking questions."

I searched him for any signs of a prank. "Warren?" I repeated as if on automatic pilot.

Ashton's expression flickered. "Okay, Connor too."

I rested my trembling hands on my lap. "Connor's been to see Krissy then." I smiled. Of course. Even though I'd been blindsided, the wheels of my brain had jumpstarted.

Ashton's jaw twitched, but he remained quiet.

"So, Krissy scares you, huh? That's what prompted this explanation." I racked my brain trying to piece together why these people teamed up and what my involvement had to do with anything. "When you say 'he' took an interest, am I to assume that means Trent? He liked me?"

Ashton's brief nod made the nausea swimming inside my stomach switch to a burning fire.

"But why did Vic, Warren, Connor, and you team up against Trent?"

Ashton jerked his head back in surprise.

"I'm not stupid, Ash."

"I never said—"

"Trent blackmailed all of you." I cut him off, tired of this charade, and more than a little upset over all of it.

He opened his mouth to speak, but I held up my hand, silencing him. "Bradley confessed to stealing exams and selling them. Connor had fallen deeply in love with Professor Fletcher. So much so that he slept with her, but unfortunately, the feeling wasn't mutual. Trent seized on it. He had proof, and he threatened to go to Krissy over it. Now, Krissy," I propped my elbows beside my full plate and studied Ashton's rigid frame, "she fought back. That ended up being her mistake, right? Nobody resisted Trent, and when she did, he had to squash her, but she held something over him. Something so heinous, I'm guessing, that it kept him in check. Momentarily, I might add. Because he had something else on her, didn't he? My question is, what? More than that, Krissy urged me to talk with you, Ash. She's locked in a jail cell for Trent's murder, and she's hellbent on me asking you for... what?"

As if in a game of chess, each taking in the other, we both sat silent. Except for the faintest of smirks, he'd masked his emotions like a champion.

"Oh," I held up a finger. "And then there's Warren's comment that's left me puzzled." I tapped my finger against my lips. "What's his sister got to do with anything?"

Ashton reached for his water glass, his hand steady. Almost too steady. It was almost as if he was contemplating what to say next. Clearly, he hadn't planned on confiding in me, but Connor's and Warren's messages had him on edge, and especially Krissy's.

Ash sipped his water before speaking. "You've been busy." He relaxed into his seat and smiled weakly.

The waiter walked over but turned on the spot and headed back for the kitchen when Ashton raised his hand, waving him off. The tension was thicker than rawhide, and even he had felt it.

"That's right. I'm here under duress." He twisted his head and tugged at his suit collar. "We never—"

"Meant to hurt me." I sighed. "Out with it. What aren't you telling me? I don't think Krissy killed Trent, and you don't either, or you wouldn't be here. Spill it."

Brothers stuck together. I had heard it countless times before, usually referring to women's indiscretions. This was much more serious than an affair or a DUI. This was murder.

Ashton leaned forward, his voice barely audible. I had to crane my ear in his direction to hear.

"Warren will kill me for this." He swore while interlacing his fingers together into a tight ball. "Warren's sister, Lila, was a beautiful, vivacious girl."

Ashton's eyes held a far-off look as he reminisced. "She could charm anyone with her big blue eyes and wit. Actually, you remind me of her." He looked down at his white knuckles. "Lila was Warren's little sister by four years. He saw her as a little pest that tagged along on everything from movies to dinners, but we didn't mind. Well, Vic and I didn't. Warren on the other hand, yeah, he wasn't amused. But that was Lila. Their parents worked, and she was Warren's responsibility. If he left her at home, the house would have burned down or she'd have joined the circus." He smiled fondly, remembering, while I remained silent. "A spitfire, she was." Ash swallowed hard, his eyes crinkling in distress. "When Warren got his acceptance to the college, we were all excited. Vic was following me, and now Warren. Being attached at the hip for all of K through 12, we were over the moon to continue the journey. We all prepared for college, each of us getting our dormitory assignments. Then Warren's dormitory roommate contacted him and asked to meet up. This was, of course, normal as you know, and we didn't think anything of it even though this guy was from New York. He seemed friendly, and he wanted to fly out, which should have been red flag number one, but we didn't think much of it. A week later Trent showed up."

Remembering Krissy's words of warning, my whole body tensed as the scene unfolded.

"He noticed Lila."

Ash nodded and roughly ran his hand through his hair. "Everyone noticed Lila, she was life itself. But that weekend..."

I breathed in deeply. The proverbial train barreled down the tracks while I sat, powerless to stop it.

"He assaulted Lila," I stated.

Ashton's faraway look evaporated. He shook his head as if to rid him of the memory. "Yes. She was never the same. Her whole demeanor changed overnight. She went from talkative and bouncy to weepy and isolated. Lila refused to eat and kept her door locked. It was only when Trent left that Victoria got her to open her door, but just to her. No other male was allowed in Lila's room. I don't need to tell you how angry we were when Vic told us a few hours later what had happened."

I waited for Ashton to continue, but he didn't. He fingered the buttery garlic bread on the edge of his plate.

"Did you call the authorities?"

"Yes, but we learned all too quickly what a big-time lawyer Trent's father was because Trent turned it around, saying Connor attacked her."

I cursed under my breath. "Figures. But why come here? Why join the same fraternity?"

"We vowed to watch him and to never let it happen again. We promised Lila." He choked up. Tears brimmed his lashes. "We failed, Kaitlynn. We failed miserably. He not only kept doing it, he started this whole rating system." Ashton's fevered gazed locked onto mine. "Please believe me when I say we tried to stop it. The police wouldn't do anything. We already knew that with Lila. Then Warren told us about the roofies, and we determined it had to *end*." Ashton slammed his fist on the table with the last word, spilling water from his glass.

I licked my dry lips. "Did you have any involvement in Trent's murder?"

His pitiful expression caused my heart to twist painfully in my chest. "Ash?" I pressed, more insistent.

"He's the one who did it," Ash blurted out.

Stunned, I stared at him with wide eyes.

"He's the one who killed Lila, Kaitlynn, and I'll never forgive myself for it."

CHAPTER 23

"*I* don't understand. Did Trent fly back sometime during school? How is he not behind bars? His father couldn't have gotten him out of that without a good fight."

Ashton swiped at the corners of his eyes. "No, there was no trial. His father didn't have to do anything other than sully Lila's good name. The humiliation, isolation, and grief took her. It was by her own hand, you see."

I stared at him straightening his tie and fighting to regain a semblance of control over his emotions. Men… they were afraid of them. Emotions were a nuisance to be buried and never to see the light of day, but they rarely ever did, especially during life's trying times.

The waiter peeked his head out from the kitchen again, and my warning stare had him scurrying back through the door.

"Ashton, what happened to Lila was unforgivable."

"Yes," he snorted. "It was, and that's exactly the point."

"I'm not following."

Ash drew in a deep breath. "Warren, Vic, and I made a pact we'd never knowingly allow Trent to hurt another female again. We stuck to him like glue. Befriended him."

"He didn't suspect anything?"

Ashton's lips curled into a snarl. "Why would he? Lila was a fleeting fancy. Once he got what he wanted, he moved on with the next shiny object, and we were prepared. When he showed interest in rushing, Warren and I rushed too. We made certain to join the same fraternity. It wasn't that hard. Warren's a chameleon. He can charm the pants off of anybody. Funny enough, it was Warren the fraternity wanted, not Trent. He's too arrogant. Warren convinced the whole group to let Trent join, and the rest is history."

"Okay, everyone joined. That doesn't explain his death, or the rating system you all have. If you're so against what Trent did, then why go along with it? Why not step in there? Come on, Ash, roofies? You expect me to believe that you had no idea about them?"

Ashton's face was chalky white. "I didn't. Not until Connor told me."

"When was that?" A group of young men dressed in our college football team jerseys jostled by, goofing off. One guy eyed me and smiled.

It was getting crowded. We needed to move this along.

"Krissy's incident," I muttered.

"He told you?" Ash asked in surprise.

"Under duress. Listen, if you only found out about the roofies, that makes you a prime suspect."

Ashton's jaw twitched. "I thought if I explained everything to you that we could move on. Together."

It was my turn to snort. "Really?"

Ashton took me in for a moment, his features stiff and angry like a volcano before erupting. This was a side I'd never witnessed, and it made my skin crawl. Was Ash capable of murder? From what I'd gathered, quite possibly he was. He had motive, and he definitely had means. Any one of his fraternity brothers could have poisoned Trent, and they were also the only ones with access to the bedrooms and the contents within practically at all waking and sleeping hours of the day and night.

"Connor had as much reason to kill him as I did. In fact, he had more."

I wrinkled my brow. "What do you mean? Krissy got away."

He laughed mirthlessly. "Is that what Connor told you? Sorry to pee in your cornflakes, but Krissy was yet another of Trent's sadistic trophies."

"But she said—" I stopped cold. It was a slip of magnanimous proportions.

Ashton rubbed the back of his neck. "Krissy told you about that? She promised—never mind. That explains a lot."

"Ashton—"

"What is this?" he barked. "Why did you really call me?"

He tossed his napkin beside his plate and stood.

"Ashton, wait!"

The cute football player that had walked by earlier zeroed in on us as I scrambled to prevent Ashton from leaving. Zipping around the table, I thrust my hands against his chest, stopping him. His heart beat wildly against my palms and I stared up into his haunted eyes.

"Don't go. Not yet. Please."

He pulled away, and my hands fell to my sides. Ashton sat, methodically laying the napkin in his lap again.

I inwardly sighed and took my seat, noticing the footballer staring intently at me. My face was hot under the scrutiny as I wracked my brain for his name. He was the star of our football program, and practically every female fawned over him. As I recalled, he had a girlfriend. A snooty cheerleader, if I'm not mistaken. Hotness wasn't enough for me. The person had to have a good soul, or it wasn't worth it, in my opinion. Ashton had it. Or at least, I thought he did.

"Ash, Krissy's in jail, charged for Trent's murder. If she didn't do it, then why not help me?"

"You?" he asked. "What can you do? Have her call a lawyer."

"You don't like Krissy."

"And you do? Come on, Kaitlynn. She's a nuisance, always wanting some kind of trinket or meal. Krissy uses Connor, and he's better off without her."

"In prison? For a crime she didn't commit?"

"And you know this how? With some Nancy Drew mumbo jumbo investigation that's gotten you what?"

I folded my arms. "Nice try, but I'm not spilling the beans, Ash. If what you've said today is true, that you like me—"

"Love."

I blinked. "Pardon?"

Ashton boldly stared back. "I love you, Kaitlynn." He shook his head in a measured fashion. "I can't tell you when it happened, but I do."

"Fine. If you really love me, then help me. Krissy is innocent, isn't she? You know something more that you're not telling me. What is it? Don't let Krissy go away for a crime she didn't commit, even if you despise the woman. That's not the Ash I fell for."

Ashton grabbed his fork and stabbed at a meatball the size of my fist. "Krissy *probably* didn't murder Trent, but Connor... He and Trent were sleeping with someone. I never figured out who, but Connor was furious. He knocked on my door one night last week and we talked about it."

"Were you surprised?"

He thought for a moment before stuffing a large chunk of meatball into his mouth. He shook his head and swallowed. "No, I guess not. What was most surprising is that it was over an older woman. Trent, I could see, but Connor's still goofy and awkward. What would an older woman see in him? Anyway, he didn't want to hurt Krissy."

"He was sleeping with an older woman, Ash. He did hurt Krissy. That's beside the point. Do you really think Connor would kill Trent over this woman? Was he that obsessed?"

Ashton shrugged and kept gnawing on a piece of bread soaked in olive oil. "Women have a way of making people do awful things," he said around a mouthful of meatball.

"What about Warren? He had motive and means."

"Nah, I don't think so." Ashton swirled his spaghetti around his fork. "The timing's off."

"The timing?" I asked, perplexed.

Ashton stopped spinning his fork. "The Fall Ball was the agreed upon date to take him down. My role was to follow him all night while Warren and Connor watched over the ladies. I never once saw Warren or Connor close to him."

"Take him down? You mean to tell me that the Alpha Pi Fall Ball was the night to get him arrested?"

Ashton didn't even blink. "Vic agreed to be the victim. She agreed to put herself in harm's way if it meant catching him in the act. The plan was to have him arrested and sully his name, making him untouchable. It went all horribly wrong."

"Ashton, what happened?"

He looked down to the spaghetti on his fork.

"Ashton," I pushed, gripping the napkin in my lap so hard my knuckles cracked.

His fork clattered to the plate. "We never meant to kill him. He was only supposed to get arrested. Please believe me, Kaitlynn."

I stared at him, shocked by what sounded like a confession. I couldn't tear my gaze away, even though I desperately wanted to. I licked my dry lips and clamped a hand over my rolling stomach. "Ashton," I croaked, "what... happened?"

"I killed him," he stated flatly. Gone were the angst and hurt, leaving only anger in its wake, marring his once beautiful face.

My mouth fell wide open.

"I killed Trent, Kaitlynn. It's me you've been hunting. I'm ready for the police. Call that detective lady of yours. Tell her I'm ready to talk."

CHAPTER 24

The roar in my ears deafened the growing crowd. Tables had filled up around us while I gaped at Ashton, shocked to the core. I searched for a justification to explain what he said, but the memories of that night remained vivid and unyielding. Ashton was always flitting away, and at the time it annoyed me. Now it all made sense. Almost.

I inhaled deeply, settling my raw nerves. A thread of something worked feverishly in my mind. Dad always likened me to a bloodhound on a trail. "Ashton, tell me how you did it."

His defiance melted away, replaced by concern. "Call the detective." He snapped his fingers, struggling to recall the name. "Uh, Shaw, right? Call Detective Shaw and have her come pick me up. I deserve it, Kaitlynn. Krissy shouldn't be sentenced to a lifetime for something I did. No one else needs to be dragged into this. Just call her."

He leaned into his seat, crossing his arms over his chest, giving me a pointed look. However, I had a nagging feeling that something wasn't right.

"How did you do it, Ash? I'll call Detective Shaw once you've told me. You owe me that much."

Ashton pressed his lips together tightly. "Alright." He leaned forward to ensure privacy. "Vic was in charge of luring him in, getting him intoxicated, which wasn't too hard considering his borderline alcoholism. I stayed hidden, promising to protect her. Our intention was to catch him before he could do anything irreparable. Initially, Trent was skeptical. He made advances toward Vic so often that he finally gave up, and her sudden change of heart left him suspicious. I overheard him questioning her about it. You see, he enjoyed the chase. Women who willingly offered themselves to him... that wasn't exciting. They had to resist. That aspect hadn't occurred to us." Ashton idly played with his straw, swirling the ice cubes in his glass. "Something changed during the night. Perhaps it was the alcohol, or maybe he just didn't care anymore. Based on our observations, he didn't... well, you know, he hadn't acted in weeks. After a few drinks, that creep put something into Vic's drink. I followed them to his room and listened at the door. Vic was supposed to use her safety word, and then I would intervene. Earlier that evening, Vic installed cameras all over his room."

On impulse, I reached out and grasped his hand. "You recorded it?"

Ashton looked longingly down at my hand before I abruptly withdrew it. "It was to be our evidence for the courts."

"Ash, that video would have been inadmissible in court, and if anything, it's probably entrapment."

He frowned. "It's enough to arrest him, right? That's all we wanted. We'd have the video, and we'd blast it over social media. Doesn't matter that they'd take it down after a while because it would show Trent for the vile human that he was. But it... it didn't work."

"What do you mean?"

"Vic didn't say the safe word. The microphone we'd put in the room didn't pick up anything, which was odd, but now that I think about it, it makes sense."

"How?"

Ashton stared blankly, his expression as impassive as stone. "He had seen through our plan. I have no idea how, but he somehow disabled the microphone, and who knows, he might have discovered the cameras as well."

My stomach churned as the room spun around me. The noise seemed to swell, resembling a swarm of roaring bees filling the restaurant. I clung to the table with a tight, white-knuckled grip.

"When I realized…" He coughed to clear his throat. "When I realized something was wrong, I tried kicking the door open, but it's harder than it looks. So I picked the lock."

Ah, the scratch marks on the outside of Trent's door then must have been from Ashton.

"I froze, Kaitlynn," he admitted, his head hanging low. "I barged in and found her unconscious on his bed, and I just froze." He slammed his fist onto the table so forcefully that it shook.

The buzz of the bustling restaurant ceased while everyone directed their attention to us.

I offered a sheepish smile as I glanced around the room, while Ash buried his head in his hands. Eventually everyone began chatting again, but the footballer who had been fixated on me throughout the night never stopped staring. Concern etched his face.

I reached over the pile of food left uneaten and gently nudged his shoulder. Since he didn't look up, I tried again, but with more force. "Ashton."

When he lowered his hands, his eyes, now red, nearly shattered me. "She was partially undressed, lying there, and I… I…"

"Hey," I said in the gentlest tone I could muster, "he's the creep. Not you. How is Victoria?"

He shook his head. "Not good. She doesn't remember much from that night, which is a relief, I suppose. We took her to the doctor that night, and fortunately nothing… um, nothing untoward happened at least."

I felt the knots in my neck and shoulders loosen a tad. "That's wonderful news,. Did they check her blood?"

He screwed up his forehead in confusion.

"I mean, did they draw labs to check for drugs in her system? That's evidence used in a court."

"She refused. Vic only wanted to go home and asked me to stay with her." His gaze shot to me. "As a friend," he hastily added.

Though a sting of jealousy needled my heart, I was beyond the anger. This whole thing began with good enough intentions, but they clearly hadn't thought this through.

"Right, so you stormed in and stopped him," I said, eager to get back to the case. "Did you hit him? I don't recall seeing any marks on his face."

"No. That scumbag looked me in the eye and smirked before leaving, but not before taunting me. Trent made remarks about Vic not being his type, but I knew better. Vic was the only thing he pursued during our freshman year, and he continued to pursue her while she and I were dating. When we discovered he was drugging women and marking them like cattle, that's when we intervened. Krissy is innocent, and I can vouch for that."

"How? Were you with Krissy the whole night? Unless you can say that, then you've got nothing."

Ashton smirked.

"What?" I asked.

"It's all on video. Connor, Vic, and I had spent the last week setting the cameras up for this event. We were certain he'd try something, and I've looked at all the video. Krissy wasn't anywhere near Trent the entire night except for one time where she shoved some pictures at him. I'm telling you, Kaitlynn, Krissy is innocent, and I can prove it."

CHAPTER 25

For a moment, I sat speechless, but I soon regained my voice.

"Ash, why haven't you given it to the detective sooner? Why leave Krissy in jail?"

Ashton swirled his glass of water around, watching the water swell and fall. "Victoria."

"She didn't want to tell the police about what happened to her," I said.

Of course not. Who wouldn't want to bury it and forget that it ever happened? This time, though, Vic could really help someone. This time there was irrefutable proof that Krissy wasn't to blame.

"Have you spoken to Victoria about it since my attack?"

Ashton sighed. "So many times I've lost count. It's difficult to convince Vic to do anything she doesn't want to, and trust me, she knows what's at stake."

"Let me ask you this, Ash. In all the videos, who was around Trent the most? Was anyone who got close to him acting weird?"

"What do you mean? Everyone pretty much steered clear of Trent. His reputation preceded him, especially when he was inebriated."

"I'm not talking about that. Did you see anyone get close enough to slip something into his drink?"

Ashton tapped his forefinger against the table. "Wait. Do you think someone poisoned him at the party?"

"I'm sure of it."

"How? Why?" His anger and shame had gradually given way to curiosity.

My phone vibrated in my purse. It was Skylar. We were running out of time. The news had just reported the preliminary autopsy findings: poison. Krissy was being transferred to a more secure facility in Denver.

I swore under my breath. "Ashton, can you send me those videos ASAP?"

"Sure, but why the rush? Don't you want the detective to get them first?"

"Send them to both of us, and if you want to keep Victoria out of this, then send them anonymously."

"Why didn't I think of that?" he mumbled, but I was up and bolting for the door. Halfway across the room, I remembered Ash. "Sorry, I've gotta run. We'll pick this up later, but send me those videos pronto."

I rushed out and into the waiting car.

"Back to the apartment," I said, fumbling with the seatbelt.

Skylar floored it. "What are we doing next?" she asked, zipping in and out of traffic.

My phone buzzed. A small smile tugged at the corners of my mouth.

"We've got videos to watch."

"Of what?" Skylar briefly glanced my direction, swerving at the last minute to avoid an elderly woman crossing the road.

"How did you...?" I wagged a finger at the woman now safely behind us.

"Intuition."

Skylar's intuition was something to behold because that elderly woman came out of nowhere. I doubt anyone else would been able to avoid crashing into her, but not Sky. Phew.

As soon as we pulled into the parking lot and rushed to my apartment, we wasted no time in reviewing the hours of video footage from that day. Everything Ashton had mentioned about Krissy was accurate, yet we were no closer to identifying the killer. The recording cut to black just as Vic approached Trent's bedroom door, holding an open can of beer in one hand. She then glanced up boldly at the camera before it conked out.

"Dang it." I flung myself backward onto my pillow and banged my head on the headboard. "Ow." I stared up at the ceiling full of glow-in-the-dark stars stuck to it. It had grown dark in the room and I admired the glow of the constellations my dad and I had positioned there, reminding me of my own room at home.

"I'm hungry," Skylar said from somewhere in the dark at the foot of the bed. "I wonder if Olivia's up."

"Why? Are you hungry for donuts?"

A whoosh of air hit my face a second before the pillow bopped me in the nose, giving me enough time to swing my arm up to soften the blow.

"Ugh," I groaned, snatching the pillow and propping it behind my head. "If you're wanting donuts so badly, why don't you call her? I'll eat anything at this point."

"Except for the spaghetti you left uneaten at the restaurant."

We'd been over this three times tonight. Skylar was perturbed that I hadn't gotten a to-go box for the meal, but I really hadn't thought about it at the time. I'd rushed out, leaving it behind, and she'd pouted ever since hearing about it. Skylar was a huge proponent of using everything and wasting nothing.

She whipped out her phone and dialed Olivia, who promised to pick up some donuts on her way over.

"She agreed too quickly." Skylar grinned. "Maybe there's hope for her after all."

"What is it with you and everybody else's love lives?" Chuckling, I reached for the remote to turn on the TV for some light, too exhausted to get up and switch on the overhead light. The first thing that appeared on the screen dampened both of our spirits.

"Why do they act like Trent was such a great person?" Skylar glared at the screen, her features pinched and drawn.

We were both exhausted from searching for clues and piecing together a picture that looked more like a horror film with each passing hour.

The videos showed Trent lurking in the shadows, sipping on alcohol with seemingly little effect. When it finally did hit him, the only obvious sign wasn't a lack of coordination but his slurred speech, and even that was slight. That failed to stop him from slugging fraternity brothers, grabbing females, or pinning an unsuspecting freshman against the wall, laughing in his brothers' faces when the women broke free.

We rewatched these moments over and over, trying to understand where the vitriol for Trent had come from.

"This doesn't add up." I absently tossed a yellow throw pillow up and down. "Trent's supposed to be the bad guy, right?"

"Yep, it's strange." Skylar snatched the pillow in mid-fall. "Stop that. It's driving me bonkers and makes it difficult to process anything."

I restarted the video and watched as Ashton stepped in, drawing Trent's anger. If memory served, this marked the third argument they had that night, with each altercation escalating in intensity until Ashton received a blow to the stomach. It was evident there was no brotherly love between those two.

When the video ended I stared up at the ceiling, mulling over the details. "Okay, Skylar. Let's go over it again. Maybe something will jog our memories and fit the final piece together."

Skylar's shoulders drooped and she flopped onto the bed. "Might as well while we're waiting. Alright, first we have Connor, Warren, and Trent in a relationship with Professor Fletcher."

"Wait. Was Warren in a relationship with the professor too? I hadn't made that connection yet."

"Uh... let me look at our notes. Hmmm... I guess not. Wonder where I got that idea?"

It wasn't a stretch, however, to imagine Warren in a relationship with her, but neither the professor nor anyone else had claimed it as truth, so it was best leaving it out for now.

"Correction. Connor and *Trent* were in a relationship with Professor Fletcher while Connor had been dating Krissy and Trent had the hots for... well, practically everyone, but especially you, Kaitlynn."

I shivered at the thought of those pictures he'd stored in his black book.

"Did you ever notice his interest?" Skylar's voice had a slightly elevated pitch, a telltale sign whenever she probed. It went against her personality of ironclad privacy, which made sense considering her less than stellar childhood of being locked in cellars for hours on end.

"Nope. Not a clue. Next." I'd rather not think about it too much because it left me queasy.

"Trent kept a black book of women on campus—or rather, *students* on campus—that he either got drunk or drugged and then tattooed, photographed, rated, and engaged in other activities with. He really should be in prison instead of in a coffin, but Ashton's correct."

"How so?" I asked.

"Men get away with it, no matter how much we stand up for ourselves. In fact, we end up being dragged through the mud and having to relive the horror countless times, while they get away with either no punishment or a slap on the wrist because heaven forbid they actually face consequences for their actions. Let's not disrupt their futures."

Her face bright red, she roughly flipped to the next page in the notebook. "It's not fair, and don't tell me again how life isn't fair because I'll... I'll scream."

I waited for her to compose herself. The truth was, I loathed the system for essentially excusing atrocious behavior. No matter how a woman dressed—whether in sweats, a potato sack, or even a cardboard box—the majority of cases would see defense attorneys attacking their characters and suggesting that they were somehow inviting trouble. It didn't matter if they were drugged. "You shouldn't have been drinking," would be the sentiment echoed in court, a sentiment upheld by many. It didn't matter that it was against their will. "You shouldn't have been out," would be another criticism, because girls should supposedly be at home, safe in bed, preserving their virtue.

Depressing? Absolutely. True? Absolutely. Women weren't afforded the luxury of ever lowering their guard because the moment they did, bad things might happen, and the blame would inevitably fall on them. As much as it pained me to acknowledge it, life was undeniably unjust. However, I refused to relinquish hope that one day men would be held accountable for their actions. Only then would women be truly liberated to live without fear. But that fight, and that hope, would have to wait for another night. Tonight, our priority was to free Krissy and finally solve this murder.

I looked up at the constellations that had soothed me as a child and marveled at how some things never changed when I spotted Ursa Major. The Big Dipper, more specifically. Although it wasn't considered a constellation in its own right, it was part of something bigger, creating a constellation seen practically any time of year in the Northern Hemisphere. Ever the stargazer, my father had pointed out the various constellations with a fervor I'd rarely seen in him to this day, and Ursa Major and Ursa Minor were his absolute favorites. In Latin, Ursa Major means "greater bear" while Ursa Minor means "lesser bear." I stared up at them now on my ceiling, yet still had a difficult time seeing the crawling bear of Ursa Major. *Bear.*

A surge of tension hit me like a downpour.

I sprang off the bed and hurried to switch on the light just as a knock sounded on the apartment door.

Skylar squinted against the sudden illumination, blinking rapidly. "I didn't realize you were so hungry."

Instead of walking out of the room to let Olivia in, I darted for the dresser and rifled through the photos we'd printed from the night of the murder. I always thought better when I could touch it, hold it up close.

"Don't worry," Skylar said behind me as I shuffled through photo after photo, ignoring the second knock, "I'll let Olivia in."

When she returned, Olivia in tow, I spun around, holding up the three burned photos from the frat house.

"What's she so giddy about?" Olivia asked, holding two boxes of donuts stacked on one hand and a tray of to go cups of coffee.

I grinned from ear to ear while they watched me like I'd gone mad.

"Follow the tattoos," I said.

"Pardon?" Skylar stepped forward, her forehead scrunched in confusion.

"The tattoos. Why didn't I think of this before? It's been staring us in the face this whole time."

Skylar took the photos while Olivia set the food down on the bed, careful not to spill our drinks.

They both studied the photos for a minute.

"A dragon, a snake, and a bear." Skylar looked from the photos to me, unsure, but Olivia seized the photos.

"Wait." She zoomed over to the other pictures. When she found the ones she wanted, she turned and held them up. "Here's more of the same. Are you saying they branded some women with their own marks?"

"Yep," I nodded, elated. The dots were finally connecting.

Skylar cocked her head. "The Chinese symbols were one thing, because anyone sobering up may regret it but it's still looks nice. These…" She shook her head.

"Exactly." I shuffled through the rest of the piles scattered on the dresser and the nightstand, picking out others until I found the exact one I'd been searching for. "Look at this one in particular. What do you see?"

Olivia and Skylar studied each in turn as I laid them out on the foot of the bed by the food, setting the zinger last.

"Kaitlynn, they're all of bears, dragons, and snakes. The women's faces aren't shown. I don't get what we're supposed to be seeing."

Skylar stayed quiet, lost in concentration, slowly making her way from one end to the other, resting finally on the last photo. She tilted the photo this way and that, then her eyes widened.

I nodded as she stared from the photo to me.

"This is Krissy, isn't it?" Skylar asked.

Olivia grabbed the photo. "What? How can you tell?"

"The dragon's tail. I remembered seeing it before, but I couldn't place it until now."

"Yeah, but Kaitlynn," Olivia pressed, "loads of women have the same dragon tattooed on various body parts. These pictures show it."

I felt the calm descend before the storm. "Yes, but not one with a blue tail."

Olivia refocused on the picture. "Oh wow."

"Ladies," I rocked back on my heels. "I believe this changes everything."

CHAPTER 26

"*E*xplain it to me one more time," Olivia said, munching on a raspberry-filled donut, some of which dribbled down her chin. Both my friends sat at the top of the bed facing me while I was perched on the foot, heart pumping faster than a hummingbird's wings.

I handed her a napkin. "Skylar and you will stay in the car a block away while I meet up—"

"With a killer?" Skylar humphed. Needless to say, she was less than thrilled with the whole idea, but we couldn't back down now. From my last call with Detective Shaw, Ashton hadn't relayed our conversation from earlier this evening, and we couldn't risk Krissy being transferred. What was weirder, was that he hadn't answered any of my texts or calls either.

"Yes, Sky, with the potential killer. I *could* be wrong."

"Not likely." Sky tidied up the pictures and stacked them neatly in piles on the bed. She liked to tidy things up when nerves hit. Once, she deep cleaned my entire apartment over a midterm. I wasn't complaining, but yikes, I'd rather take a walk or watch a funny movie than dust or do laundry.

"Stay in the car, alright? I'll enter through the front and wait for them to show. The phone will be on the entire time. If you hear anything you don't like, call the police and make sure to mention Detective Shaw."

My friends stared at me, their postures rigid and faces drawn. A part of me wavered, wanting to throw in the towel immediately, but the information we had wasn't enough for the police to take us seriously. With Krissy to be hauled off to a higher security prison in less than twelve hours, we were out of other options.

"I don't like it." Skylar huffed, crossing her arms against her chest. "It's too dangerous."

"I agree with Sky," Olivia said, rubbing her sticky fingers on the napkin. "However, I don't see any other way. So... I'm in."

"Great." I clapped my hands together. "Let's get dressed."

TWENTY MINUTES LATER, we were creeping at a snail's pace up to the burned out light post closest to the frat house. I came to a halt and engaged the squeaky parking brake. The night was unusually still. Not even the leaves moved.

"I don't like this," Skylar protested yet again. "Something's *not* right."

"Spidey senses tingly again?" Olivia smiled from the backseat, her teeth sparkling white in the moonlight.

Skylar pressed her hand against the cool glass beside her. "Nothing's moving, Kaitlynn. Not a branch, a leaf, a car, or animal. That's not usual."

Sky was right. Something felt off in the mountain air, but I wasn't about to admit it for fear she'd beg me to let the police handle it.

"She's right," Olivia agreed, nose to the cool glass, her breath fogging it all up. "Why aren't there people out and about on a party night?"

"There's been a murder," I said. "That kind zaps the fun out of things."

I stared through the windshield at the house looming in the

moonlit sky. The police tape remained around the front yard, but the guys had ripped it from the main walkway.

I gripped the steering wheel with my leather-gloved hands and breathed in to a count of three. "Alright, here goes."

Without further consideration, I exited the car and set off, tucking my hands into my jacket pockets, merging into the darkness with my all-black attire. I stayed in the shadows until I arrived at an open area devoid of trees and bushes. It would only be for a few seconds, but it would expose me to anyone watching.

"Here goes nothing," I whispered.

I launched into the open, walking to the door, white puffs floating up with each breath. I nervously glanced up at the windows and the surrounding area. My eyelids were twitching with tension when I finally made it to the front door.

I stumbled up the front step and reached for the handle, only blowing out the air I'd been holding once safely inside. In the foyer, I strained my eyes in the dark, waiting for them to adapt.

It was odd that the lights were out, and I wanted to turn tail and run. Yet I stood firm and made my way up the stairs to my left.

The ballroom was empty of all chairs and tables, except for the table holding the coffin. It was back in an open room with an elaborate crystal chandelier hanging from the center. The wooden floors creaked underfoot, announcing my presence to anyone within proximity.

I froze. Straining to hear, I waited for one... two... then three seconds. Then I trudged forward into the ballroom lit only by the moonlight outside streaming in through the tall windows.

"Why here?" someone rumbled at me from behind. The words echoed off the walls and high ceiling.

Heart pounding against my ribcage, I turned.

"You came," I said, locking my knees to keep them from shaking harder.

The only exit was blocked by his imposing figure, I swallowed down my fear and met his confident gaze head-on.

"How could I resist?" He smirked, hands nonchalantly tucked into his pockets. "When Warren is summoned, Warren appears."

Normally invoking the third-person reference would be irritating, but tonight, under the cloak of darkness, it was downright eerie.

"Or should I address you as 'bear'?" I countered, standing tall with my shoulders squared. I jutted out my chin and noticed the smirk fade. Ah, I had struck a nerve. A vulnerability, so to speak.

"Only my girlfriend calls me that."

"Why is that, Warren?"

He began to advance toward me, his movements deliberate, reminiscent of a cat, smooth and graceful. By the time he responded, he was close enough for me to detect the scent of alcohol emanating from him.

"Oh, I believe you're familiar with it, Katydid. Do you mind if I use that nickname?" His grin widened, a mischievous glint flickering in his eyes.

"Is that your Dungeons and Dragons character?" I stood my ground, rigid, while Warren leisurely circled around me. The gentle click of his soles echoed with each step.

"Why?" His whisper startled me, mere inches from my ear, close enough for me to prickle against the warmth of his breath on my cheek. "Wanna play, Katydid?"

He pulled away.

I silently breathed out when he came into focus again.

The exit had been in view, and he'd actually given me the chance to run, but I remained fixed in my spot. I hadn't gotten evidence recorded yet.

I fingered my cell in my pocket, hoping it recorded clearly through the thin material. I'd worn this especially for the occasion, even though it barely kept the chill out.

Now back where he started, Warren loomed larger than his usual 6'5" height in the darkness. A wicked smirk twisted his lips.

"I'm not interested in Dungeons and Dragons, only the characters that you, Connor, and Ashton played."

He barely blinked, his focus solely on me and my unease. "Why is that, my dear?"

Warren took a single step closer, but with his long stride, it seemed more like a leap.

I flinched involuntarily at the sudden movement, though I remained rooted to the spot.

No fear. Skylar and Olivia are right outside, ready to call the cops. I can handle this!

"Connor's the dragon," I blurted out, my voice strained.

A grin spread across his face, reminiscent of the Cheshire Cat's. "His fascination with dragons is beyond me and rather worn out, don't you think?" He cocked his head, looking almost robotic in his movements. "It's Dungeons and *Dragons*. Please, be more original." Warren took another step forward.

I swallowed hard, my legs trembling, but I maintained eye contact with his intense gaze, illuminated by the light streaming through the arched windows.

"So he was the blue dragon?" A desperate urge to flee was rising within me.

"Come now, Katydid." The endearing nickname Ashton often used when uttered by Warren sounded more like a predator stalking its prey. "That's not what you witnessed. Warren doesn't tolerate falsehoods."

"I-I'm not lying," I stammered.

"Wrong!" He snapped, sending a jolt of fear through my racing heart. "Think again, Katydid. Your very life depends on it."

I tried to remember the picture, but his proximity disrupted any coherent thought.

"What a pity." He tsked. "I thought you were smarter than that, Katydid. Ash spoke of your intelligence and wit, but sadly, I see none, and your usefulness to me is over."

"Wait!" I thrust out a hand as he reached inside his coat pocket. "It was a green dragon with a blue tail."

A small smile perched on his lips. He dropped his hand from his pocket. Empty.

I let out a sigh of relief as the pieces of the puzzle began to fall into place.

"Time's ticking, Katydid," he pressed, taking the final long stride to stand directly in front of me.

I flinched, my gaze fixed on his torso until I raised my head, meeting his twisted grin. "You're the bear," I whispered. I licked my dry lips, silently praying that every word was being recorded and that the police were just outside the door. "Trent was the snake."

"You really did your homework. I'm impressed, Katydid."

"Homework?"

Each of us locked onto the other. Motionless, but ready to pounce or run, whatever the occasion wrought.

Warren lowered his chin, his eyes appearing solid black in the dim light. "Can't you see, Katydid? I left you those clues. I *wanted* you to find them."

A surge of bile stung the back of my throat as I swallowed hard against the knot that had formed. "Why?"

Warren didn't have a chance to respond. A loud thwack behind me made me spin around. I rushed to the coffin as something inside thrashed and kicked, causing it to shift a few inches on the table, threatening to topple over at any moment.

Turning back, I searched for Warren, but he had vanished, his voice echoing ominously overhead like a specter.

"I've prepared a gift for you, Katydid," echoed throughout the ballroom.

I seized the coffin lid and pulled. It was securely bolted shut.

"Are you there?" I shouted near the lid.

The thrashing intensified as I clawed at the opening. I wiggled, pulled, and wiggled again, inching the lid open until it flew backward, sending me tumbling to the ground. I regained my footing and peered down into the dark coffin.

I gasped. "Ash?"

CHAPTER 27

$\mathcal{T}$he reverberation of manic laughter permeated the ballroom through strategically positioned loudspeakers, creating the illusion of being trapped in a dungeon.

"Ash, hold on," I urged.

I yanked off the cloth gagging him.

"Hurry, Kaitlynn," he gasped, blood oozing from his mouth and nose. "He's insane. He's lost his mind."

I untied the rope binding his wrists just as Warren's voice echoed again.

"Find the dragon, Katydid. Find the dragon, and you'll get your reward."

The last of the rope around his ankles fell away and Ashton scrambled out. I braced the table to prevent it from tipping, and soon he stood on his own two feet, bent over and panting, his crimson-caked palms planted on his thighs while he inhaled deeply.

I bent close to his ear, rubbing his back. "Ash, do you know where Connor is? Where did he put him?"

Ashton clasped a hand to his chest, his face contorted in pain. "He...he hit us... with something. I-I tried stopping him... Connor ra-ran at him, b-but he got h-hit on t-the head... w-with a shovel."

My blood ran cold. "Is there a secret room in this building? Think, Ash."

Ashton struggled to stand upright, his hand still pressed against his shirt, stained crimson. He gestured for me to follow him toward the exit of the ballroom.

I scanned the rafters, the darkened corners of the room, searching for any sign of Warren's looming figure.

We ran down the stairs, Ashton pointing shakily toward the kitchen entrance. "There," he gasped. He staggered forward, hunched over and clutching his abdomen.

"Let me take a look," I said, placing my hand on his shoulder.

"I'm fine," he insisted, attempting to straighten up but swaying in place, clearly in pain.

"No, you're not."

I squinted in the dim light, seeing the crimson stain had spread across his abdomen and now crawled further up his torso.

"Ash, you need a doctor," I whispered, acutely aware we were more than likely being watched and probably recorded.

"Leaving so soon?" Warren's voice echoed through the room, sending a chill down my spine.

A click drew my attention to the front door, where the deadbolt had just been locked. Throughout the house, I could hear the same clicks resounding.

"I tried being civil, but apparently you need a bit of motivation. Let the games commence. Find Connor within the next ten minutes or he'll meet his end. The countdown starts now."

With grim determination, Ashton struggled toward the kitchen entrance, each step a painful effort as he dragged himself forward, his legs heavy as lead.

I maneuvered past him and held the swinging door open as he entered, my eyes searching the shelves stocked with pots, pans, and bags of flour and pasta. The only semblance of illumination came from the overhead emergency lights. One hung above the serving station, casting a faint glow over the dining area, while another loomed directly above us, casting unsettling shadows that accentuated

Ashton's haggard appearance. His eyes were sunken, his skin clammy and pallid, and his exaggerated blinks seemed to occur in slow motion, as if he were in a drunken stupor. If we didn't locate Connor and find a way out of here within the next few minutes, I feared for both Ashton's and Connor's safety.

Grabbing the nearest cloth from a neatly arranged stack of folded napkins on the supply rack to my left, I approached Ashton with my hands raised. "I need to stop the bleeding."

He nodded and placed a hand on my shoulder while I bent to inspect the wound. Gently pulling back his shirt, I noticed the ragged hole in it, and blinked back the tears that sprang to my eyes. Behind the sticky, soaked cloth, his abdomen rapidly rose and fell, pushing more blood out of the jagged wound.

"This will hurt," I whispered, glancing up at his pale face.

He clenched his lips tightly and shut his eyes, his other hand steadying himself on the nearest rack. "Go for it."

I applied the cloth against his wound and grabbed another. He drew in a sharp breath, but admirably, stayed silent. After applying two cloths, the bleeding began to slow.

"I need to find something to secure this." When I moved to turn away, his grip tightened on my shoulder.

"No," he rasped, his voice strained and low. "We need to find Connor. He's...he's..."

"You have to keep pressure on the wound."

He released my shoulder and pressed down firmly on my hand. I withdrew mine from beneath his, and we continued through the kitchen toward the back door. Connor was nowhere in sight. Either he was hiding exceptionally well or had been stowed away in a refrigerator or freezer, because after a few more minutes, we had thoroughly examined every corner.

"What now?" I inquired. "Is there another exit from here besides the one leading to the backyard? Perhaps a basement door?"

Ash shook his head with visible effort. "No," he replied hoarsely. "But there's a closet. Over there."

He motioned to a six-foot metal rack full of spices to the left of the back door. I lifted the side of it and slid it out of our way, noting the knob, and pulled it wide. A rush of dust flew out, and a moldy, sour smell knocked me back a foot, crashing into Ashton and sending him stumbling backward into the kitchen island.

"Sorry!" I yelped. I looked down and let out a shriek. "Connor!"

I lunged forward and dropped to my knees beside his motionless form, crumpled on the floor.

"Connor? Can you hear me?" I asked, gently tapping his cool yet sweaty cheeks.

Connor's head moved ever so slightly as he groaned, his eyes tightly shut.

Was it pain? Fear? Perhaps both, but with Warren lurking nearby, we couldn't afford to linger. How were we supposed to proceed with two injured men? And with Warren's unpredictable presence adding to the mix, the situation was dire.

Ash clung to the doorway, his head bowed, looking down at Connor with furrowed brows. "He drugged him and knocked him out, Kaitlynn. He's not moving anytime soon."

"Right you are!"

We both snapped our heads toward Warren's triumphant voice.

I recoiled when the light flicked on, shielding my eyes with my hand. The sudden brightness stung, making my eyes water.

"What did you drug him with?" I demanded, my patience wearing thin.

"Well, well," he tutted, glancing over at Ashton, who leaned heavily against the wall. He swayed for a moment before steadying himself. "She's got spirit, doesn't she?"

Warren closed the distance between us in an instant.

My breath hitched when he seized my chin in his leather-clad hand. "You would have been his masterpiece," he snarled, shoving me roughly. I spread my arms wide, gripping the closet doorframe to avoid stepping on Connor still sprawled on the closet floor.

"And you," Warren advanced on Ashton. He retrieved something from behind his back and I caught the glint of a gun. He pressed the butt beneath Ashton's jaw.

Ashton squeezed his eyes shut as his head collided with the kitchen wall.

"Warren," I said, my voice low but firm, "put the gun away." I prayed my friends had contacted the police because this had escalated from creepy to dangerous. I wondered why they hadn't arrived yet. Warren's behavior had been reckless, but hearing Ashton had been hurt should have prompted them to call the cops. Since they hadn't shown up, I had no other options.

"Warren," I repeated, rising slowly, palms facing him in a gesture of surrender. "You don't want to do this."

"Don't I?" He pressed the gun harder against Ashton's chin. "Tell her!"

"Tell me what?" I asked.

"Tell her, Ash, or so help me—"

"Fine." Ashton cut him off. "It was my idea."

"What?" I asked, my gaze darting between Ashton's grimace and Warren's murderous grin.

"I thought this whole thing up," Ashton admitted, his voice strained.

I stood staring at them. Ashton, helpless against the wall, and Warren's murderous grin nose to nose with him.

"Say it!" Warren shouted, spittle flying out of his mouth. He was in anguish and had lost his mind, but I wasn't connecting something. What was I missing? "Say it or I pull the trigger."

"Hey," I said, keeping my voice light, but my knees wobbled beneath me, threatening to give way. "Maybe he'd be more inclined to talk if you lowered the gun, Warren."

Warren glanced at me, and I tried smiling, but the corners of my mouth felt frozen in place.

I swallowed hard, my mouth dry as cotton, speaking in a soothing tone, reminiscent of a mother coaxing a child away from danger. "You're angry—" I began.

"Angry doesn't even begin to describe it," he cut in, his voice cracking with emotion. His gaze remained fixed on Ashton. "Tell her, or I'll pull the trigger."

Warren maintained pressure with his gloved hand against Ashton's throat, keeping the gun aimed at nose level.

Ashton's pained expression morphed into a smirk. "Big mistake."

Warren's sneer turned to surprise.

In a swift motion, Ashton seized Warren's wrist holding the gun and twisted.

The sound of bones cracking echoed then a scream tore through the room.

I gasped, stunned by the turn of events.

The gun slipped from Warren's hand, landing with a clatter on the floor.

My mouth hung open in shock as I watched the scene unfold before me. Ashton now held the gun, his expression steely as he aimed it at Warren, who was curled up, cradling his injured wrist against his abdomen.

"Ashton…" His cold, unyielding gaze silenced me, sending a chill down my spine. "No," I pleaded, tears welling in my eyes as I looked at the man I loved. "Please, no."

"He's a monster," Warren murmured.

"No," Ashton corrected. "I'm the snake."

CHAPTER 28

*A*shton subdued Warren against the wall beside me, holding the gun firmly, his attention fixed on both of us, disregarding the groans coming from the floor. The sole comfort came from the fact that Connor remained unconscious, hopefully unaffected by the chaos unraveling around us. As for Warren and me, our fate was uncertain.

"I don't get it," I said, mentally retracing the evidence we had meticulously gathered. Every photograph, every story of the tattooed women, the connection between Warren's sister and Trent. What had eluded me? Then, like a bolt of lightning illuminating a dark sky, it dawned on me. The cufflink in Connor's closet.

"It's all a setup," I whispered, my hand flying to cover my mouth in astonishment. I gazed at Ashton with widened eyes, his grin shining in response.

"Thatta girl. I sensed you could do it. Since the day we met, I *sensed it*, Kaitlynn."

"What?" I exclaimed.

"How incredibly smart you are, of course. I liken myself to a modern-day Sherlock Holmes, and so far," he tapped the butt of his gun to his temple as Warren gave up the fight and slumped against the wall, "I've gotten away with... well, let's say a lot. And Warren's sister, wow. She was a fighter, that one."

I slammed a hand on Warren's chest at the first flinch forward. If we were to get out of this alive, I needed Ash to spill his guts, not start shooting. Time for justice would arrive. Hopefully soon.

I looked at the bright red exit sign above the kitchen door leading to the foyer. Where were the cops for Pete's sake?

Ashton followed my gaze with a subtle shift of his body. Meeting my eyes again, his once-charming smile now seemed like a chilling omen. "Such a shame, really. Those pretty friends of yours."

A surge of fury ignited in my belly, causing my nails to dig into my palms. "Stay away from my friends," I spat, my words laced with restrained anger as I took a step forward.

"Kaitlynn, don't." Warren's weak protest met with deaf ears.

"Ah, feeling courageous, are we?" Ashton chuckled in an unsettling way. "I wouldn't advise it."

My eyes darted around the room, landing on the cast-iron skillet.

"Go ahead, Kaitlynn," Ashton urged, his voice ominously calm. "That skillet won't do much against a bullet, despite what movies suggest. Trust me. I've tested it."

"What have you done to my friends?"

Ashton shrugged nonchalantly. "Nothing permanent. Yet." He gestured with the gun for me to return to Warren's side.

A plan formed in my mind. It was risky, but desperate times called for desperate measures. *No risk, no reward,* as my mother always used to say.

Feeling a sense of calm as the plan took shape, I met Ashton's gaze directly. "Ash?" I said with a sweetness usually reserved for lovers, catching him off guard with the change in my demeanor. "What really happened to Warren's sister?"

I edged forward another step as his eyes narrowed. If the bullet failed to kill me, then my exploding heart would.

He hadn't noticed my uneasiness and opened his mouth to answer. He hopped up on the kitchen island, confident he had both Warren and me where he wanted and waved his gun again at me. "You're the brains. What's your hypothesis, Watson?"

Ah, there it was. I played the role of Watson, the clever yet somewhat overshadowed sidekick. Just like in fiction, I had been utilized as a muse, a fact that Ashton relished as he grinned wider at what he perceived as my realization. Little did he know that I had devoured all of Sherlock Holmes's adventures and even indulged in some fan fiction. I was more than capable of navigating this situation, if only I could inch closer to the cast-iron skillet. In this moment, I couldn't help but wonder, what would Sherlock do? Better yet, what would Sir Arthur Conan Doyle do?

I eyed the skillet, not hiding it from Ashton, which earned me yet another chuckle.

"If you want to, then by all means go for it. It's your funeral. And Warren's."

I raised a brow. "And Connor?"

Ashton frowned, as if he'd forgotten Connor's existence as a pile on the floor. "He'll toe the line," he said, but with less assurance.

"What if he doesn't?" I countered, inching closer to the skillet now that Ashton wasn't paying as much attention to me.

"Connor is a good boy. He does as he's told."

"Really?" I asked. Another big step and I'd have the skillet. I cupped my trembling hands behind me and smiled at Ash. "Like when he had that affair with Professor Fletcher? Or when he planted those pictures in Trent's drawer? Oh, right. That *was* planned, but his falling in love with the teacher is a little overdone, don't you think?"

"Hmmm. My thoughts exactly. Hearts will only get you hurt."

I placed my hand on the makeshift island adjacent to where Ashton perched, my gaze unwaveringly fixed on him. My fingers itched to grasp the skillet, but I reminded myself to remain patient.

Ashton had already indirectly implicated Connor, a deduction based on the chaotic events orchestrated by Olivia, Skylar, and me. Their attempts to deflect blame onto each other suggested a coordinated effort to divert suspicion, and unfortunately, it had been somewhat successful.

I cocked my head slightly. "But Trent... he wasn't too happy to find out he'd been stooped by you all. I'd say he was more than furious when he found out Connor had slept with his woman. Trent was never interested in me, he only had eyes for teacher."

"Ah, splendid, my dear Watson," Ashton remarked, entranced.

Though he still held the gun trained on me, his stance was casual, and his finger remained off the trigger.

I subtly edged my fingers closer to the skillet, mindful of the limited time before our conversation circled back to the silent agreement to dispose of Warren and me.

"The letters..." I puckered my lips, thinking back on the lies we'd been told, piecing together a different plot. From Krissy's altercation with Trent at the party and the taunting of the name Mercedes, I latched onto the first thing that popped to mind.

"Mercedes Fletcher."

"What about her?" Ashton asked, crossing his legs, grinning from ear to ear. He propped his elbow of the hand holding the gun on his thigh and eagerly awaited my reply.

"Those letters Krissy shoved at Trent weren't something about her blackmailing him, were they?"

"Ah!" he breathed in excitement, akin to a child in a candy store. "This is becoming quite intriguing. Wouldn't you agree, Bear?" He glanced at Warren, who observed us both warily.

"No," I pressed on, "those were Connor's letters to Mercedes."

Ashton grinned. "Excellent deduction."

"Trent's response was a veiled jab, but did he drug Professor Fletcher? Or was it..." I turned my gaze to the motionless figure in the kitchen closet. There was a subtle twitch, imperceptible yet undeniable. "Of course." When I faced Ashton again, his features had hardened, and as the light played off his cheekbones, he appeared more sinister by the minute. How did I ever see goodness in him?

"Connor drugged her, didn't he? Professor Fletcher thought it was Trent, but..." The idea formulated in my mind's eye.

"The wheels are finally turning," Ashton taunted. "It's like I can actually see them spinning in your head. Marvelous."

I briefly glanced at Connor still lying motionless on the floor. "It wasn't Trent who assaulted Mercedes Fletcher or threatened her with the board. Gosh, it wasn't even Trent's tattoo on her, was it? It's—"

"Connor's!" Ashton crowed, his glee barely contained. "Yes, I thought it was a stroke of brilliance, leading Mercedes to believe that Trent could commit such atrocities. Actually, Connor proved quite useful. He's been obsessively infatuated with her since the day he first laid eyes on her in algebra class. With him so fixated on her, I figured I might as well capitalize on it."

"But... why Trent? Why accuse him of such heinous deeds? Why fabricate the story about him assaulting Warren's sister?"

Ashton leaped off the stovetop in one fluid motion, thrusting the butt of the gun against my chest. "He took her away from me," he sneered, his face contorted in a fit of rage. Blue blood vessels bulged from his temples, and a flush of red dotted his cheeks.

My back pressed against the cool metal rack atop the small kitchen island as I held my breath, anticipating the shot.

"She was perfect. She was sweet." Ashton's gaze drifted downward, lost in a distant memory. "I needed her complete attention, but Trent..." He licked his lips roughly. "She couldn't take her eyes off him. Hanging on his every word. It was disgusting. I was there for her when her parents divorced." He was leaning in so close our noses nearly touched, his hot breath warming my cheek. "She was meant to be mine." His voice cracked.

"Oh my gosh." I stared at him, mouth agape. "You *loved* her."

The anguish etched on his face spoke volumes. He didn't need to confirm it. It was written in every line of his expression. "You didn't hurt her."

"I would never!" he yelled so close to my face that my ears rang.

I shut my eyes tight against his anger, reopening them a moment later to find he'd stepped back.

He ran a hand through his thick hair, his gaze fixed on Connor. "Trent stole her from me. He took what was mine, and when he discarded her affections..." He choked up. A solitary tear trickled down his cheek.

"She took her own life," I whispered. "When Trent showed no interest, I mean."

Ashton nodded. "I will *never* forgive him."

"So you took the only thing that mattered to him... Mercedes Fletcher. And his life." I openly gazed at him as Warren squeezed his eyes shut, tears shimmering on his face. "And you, Warren, you joined the fraternity for what?"

Warren wiped his face with the back of his hand and straightened to his full height. "Connor tried... he tried to... you know, but I walked in. Trent was there that weekend. He offered her comfort and nearly beat Connor to death, and she fell for him." Warren raised a hand when I raised a brow. "Oh no. Trent was the perfect gentleman throughout the entire ordeal. He called her to make sure she was okay for months afterward, and he even got his father to help with a lawyer, but..."

"You joined with Trent, didn't you? Alpha Pi?" I asked. The muscles in my body tightened so hard my back ached. It was all coming together, complete with a neat red bow, and what I saw was anything but pretty.

Ashton's reddened face shifted from Warren to me. "Is it all clear now, Watson?" he taunted.

"Not quite. I understand why you joined the fraternity. There are plenty of women on campus who enjoy a good frat party, and you were more than willing to join, seeing it as your hunting ground for the despicable things you do."

"Careful," he warned, his harsh tone reverberating off the walls.

"Krissy was the scapegoat."

"Yawn." He feigned boredom, patting his mouth. "Tick tock goes the clock, or I shoot."

"I'm not done yet. It was *you* who convinced the brothers to rate all the women, tattoo them, and it was also you who had Connor drug Professor Fletcher, handing Trent the bottle to give to her where then he slept with her, taking all those lewd photos, but she thought it was Trent, and cut him off. This, of course, thrilled you, except Connor became too enthralled with Fletcher, and Krissy found out—"

In my periphery, a flash of movement caught my attention, but not fast enough. A body slammed into me, banging my head onto the metal cabinet above the kitchen island. I steadied the buzzing in my head by pressing my hands against my temples. Pain shot through my right hip, making me grimace. Squinting through blurry vision, I tried to make out what pinned me down.

"Connor?" I gasped, fighting to break free. "Let me go!"

"No," he hissed. "You're the one who put Krissy behind bars. *You.* And now you'll pay."

CHAPTER 29

"*M*e?" I managed to choke out.

Connor seized a handful of my hair and pulled hard. A scream tore from my throat at the searing agony.

Ashton's maniacal laughter spurred Connor on even more. My neck throbbed from the strain as he yanked my head back, bringing his enraged face inches from mine.

"Connor," I gasped, struggling to draw breath at the awkward angle. Stars danced before my eyes. "I c-can't b-b-breathe."

"Good. You deserve to suffer. Krissy wouldn't be behind bars if you hadn't instructed her to set up the cake."

The photo of Krissy at the party with the knife hovered above the cake sprang to mind.

"What to do? *What to do?*" Ashton tsked.

The sound of two feet hitting the kitchen tile alerted me to his movement, but I couldn't see anything other than Connor's ugly mug.

"How about a game of cat and mouse?" Ashton's voice echoed. I could hear his footsteps drawing nearer. "Connor here will release you."

Connor whipped his head to Ashton. "But—"

"Silence!" Ashton commanded. "Let her go. Now."

I stumbled backward when Connor released his grip. I collided with the countertop and utensils scattered off the island and clattered to the floor. Amidst their laughter, I discreetly gripped the cool skillet handle behind my back.

"Here's how the game works," Ashton ambled over to Warren against the opposite wall in front of me and shoved the gun to his nose. Warren's skin looked pale and sweat dripped from his brow. "You two will have a ten second lead to find those girls. Only ten seconds, so let's not waste it. After that, both Connor and I race to find you."

Ashton pivoted to face me, his features contorted into a sinister grin. "I won't stop firing until all of you are *dead*," he declared, lunging forward when he uttered the last word.

I tightened my grip on the skillet and jerked backward.

"You can do whatever you want to Bear, but leave Kaitlynn to me, alright?" Ashton trailed the gun down the side of my face, his breath hot against my clammy skin.

Stepping back, he awaited Connor's nod, his gaze never leaving me.

"Right," Connor confirmed, ejecting the gun's magazine into his hand. It contained approximately fifteen bullets. "On your marks..."

With a trembling grip, I held the skillet behind me, poised to act. Glancing at Warren's pallid face, I saw him bracing against the wall with one hand and one foot.

"Get set..."

I tightened my grip on the handle, sweat making my palm slippery. "Go!" I shouted.

Warren lurched toward the kitchen exit like a bolt of lightning just as Connor took off after him. I jerked the skillet above my head and brought it crashing down onto Connor's skull with all my might. He crumpled to the floor like a sack of potatoes. Ashton swung the gun toward me, but I leaped over Connor's prone form, swinging the skillet again. The sound of metal on metal echoed through the room.

FLASH! POW!

I hit the tile floor with a thud, pain shooting through my right side.

My lungs felt constricted and I struggled for air as I scrambled to my feet and grabbed a soup pot from the ones hanging above the stove.

"You'll pay for that," Ashton's voice roared from somewhere behind me.

I spun around, snatching a knife in my other hand, and lunged toward Ashton's bent form as he reached for the gun on the floor.

His fingers touched the sleek black handle.

I thundered ahead, taking one step, then another, then another.

Ashton straightened and grinned. "You should have run."

I was too far away.

I dove for the giant bags of flour on the floor to the right, squeezing my eyes shut, bracing for the pain. Landing behind the bags stacked two feet high, I hunkered down, my knees bruised, frantically looking around for an exit or weapon.

"Come on out, Kaitlynn. It's over."

My heart raced at breakneck speed, pumping blood through my veins in a frantic rhythm. Gasping for breath, I cautiously looked over the stack of flour.

Warren's towering figure loomed over Ashton and Connor, the black gun in his right hand aimed directly at them.

"Warren?" My voice trembled. "How did you—"

"I circled back when I realized you weren't behind me. Thanks for the distraction, by the way."

A surge of relief flooded my already frazzled emotions, and I burst out laughing. At first, it was a normal laugh, but it soon escalated into hysterical laughter as I doubled over, clutching my aching abdomen. We had both narrowly escaped death.

"Hey, Kaitlynn," Warren said in a soothing tone, "it's okay. You're okay. I've got them, but I really need you to call the cops. Can you do that?"

I planted my palms on the flour bags and breathed in a deep, cleansing breath, coughing on plumes of white flour floating upward.

"The cops, Kaitlynn. Please tell me you have a phone on you."

My phone.

I dug into my pocket and pulled it out, noting the screen. Olivia and Skylar's faces beamed at me as my screensaver. I pressed the emergency tab.

"911. What's your emergency?"

The events that followed were a blur as we provided our information. The sounds of cop car sirens filled the air, and soon enough, uniformed officers stormed the house. They confiscated Warren's gun while paramedics attended to Ashton and Connor. Other medics took care of Warren and me, wrapping us in blankets once they determined our wounds were minor. We were pulled aside for questioning, but I insisted on knowing about Olivia and Sky. Only after they were found stuffed in Warren's dorm room closet, their mouths gagged and limbs bound with duct tape, did I agree to cooperate. They, too, were questioned. However, it wasn't until the arrival of a mousy brown-haired detective, who walked in and dramatically removed her shades like a character from a Bond film, that I fully regained my senses.

Seated on a plush couch in the lounge area, I experienced a sense of déjà vu. Just days ago, we were all being questioned about Trent's death, and now I found myself sinking into the couch with a feeling of shame. I had allowed Ashton and others to deceive me into believing Trent was some kind of predator who preyed on women and girls, and now the truth had come to light. Well, part of it had.

Detective Shaw settled into the worn sofa chair opposite me, her elbows resting on her slender thighs. She held a notepad in one hand and a pen in the other, her gaze taking in my disheveled appearance. "You've had quite a night, Ms. Dahl," she remarked, tilting her head slightly with an air of contemplation. "Tell me, how did we end up here?"

Her tone was devoid of blame or agitation, only curiosity evident in her voice. No accusation. No frustration. Only curiosity resonated in her voice.

"Trent..." I swallowed back tears that threatened to overflow.

Detective Shaw retrieved a napkin from somewhere within her jacket and extended it to me.

"Thank you." I used the napkin to dab at the corners of my eyes.

"Trent wasn't a bad guy. He didn't prey on women. They wanted everyone to believe that he did."

The detective's attentive gaze locked onto mine. "They?"

"Ashton and Connor. They're the real culprits."

"Please continue," she urged.

"It all began when they got accepted to college..." I relayed the details as succinctly as possible.

When I was done, she pursed her lips together, inhaling deeply. "Let me get this straight." She jabbed her pen to the notepad. "Ashton wanted a relationship with Warren's little sister, but Connor attacked her?"

"Yes."

"They both wanted her then." Detective Shaw wrote something down. "Okay, so instead of taking his vengeance out on Connor, he turned against Trent, who had consoled the girl, followed him to campus, and plotted to kill him, setting it up to appear like he started the rating system with women, drugging them, tattooing them, and abusing them. Is that right?"

"To my knowledge, yes." I wrapped the blanket tighter around my shivering shoulders. Everything ached, and as the adrenaline wore off, my eyelids grew heavy.

Detective Shaw sat ramrod straight and put her pen and notepad away in a pocket. "I've got Professor Fletcher's contact information, which I'll follow up on, but I'll need you and your friends to make a formal statement tomorrow morning at the station."

She stood, smoothing her jacket and adjusting her tie. Looking down at me, she sighed. "Next time, Ms. Dahl, leave the detective work to the trained professionals, alright?" She extended her hand, and after a moment's hesitation, I shook it.

She smiled. "You've got quite the knack for sleuthing, Ms. Dahl. Ever considered a career in criminal justice?"

I stared at her, taken aback.

"It's not as far-fetched as it sounds. You have natural talent. Something you can't teach. Think about it." With that, she turned and began to walk away, but paused after a few steps. "Good job, Ms. Dahl."

I watched her leave, her confident stride and commanding presence taking the last of my energy with her. I slumped against the couch and rested my head against the cushion. The ceiling fan whirled overhead, kicking up dust and a smell of rotting onions.

"Hey, girl."

Skylar flopped beside me, and Olivia sat where Detective Shaw was. Olivia leaned over and rubbed my aching knee.

"Ouch." I flinched. "That's definitely bruising."

Olivia smiled. "That or your pride?"

I puffed out my cheeks. "Mostly pride. I should have let the police handle this. I'm so sorry." I rubbed at my burning eyes.

"Stop," Skylar chided. She rested her head on my shoulder.

"Ouch!" I added, trying to lighten the mood.

Skylar glanced up at me. "Is there anywhere safe around here?"

"Probably not, but that's okay. Ladies," I said proudly, looking at my friends, "we did it."

"Yeah," said Olivia, "but how exactly? Skylar and I are still in the dark about how you figured it all out."

I glanced between Olivia and Sky. "I can't wait to tell you. I'd *love* to fill you in, but can we tidy up first?"

Olivia grinned and sprang to her feet. "I know just the place."

CHAPTER 30

The hot coffee slid down my throat and settled in my belly, warming me from within. I gripped the mug between my hands, reveling in its warmth. After the adrenaline from what happened waned, it left me shaken, my teeth chattering. Rightly so, according to my mother, but I detected a hint of pride in my father's Norwegian accent.

Skylar and I sat side by side, observing Olivia by the donuts, twirling her hair around her finger, captivated by Barry. They were knee deep in a conversation, probably about some scientific thing because that's usually what got Olivia's juices flowing. It was marvelous seeing her so happy, especially after what I'd dragged her through tonight.

"Good thing Ash and Conn are behind bars," Skylar said, gesturing with her mug, "or Barry would snap them in two." She smirked.

"I expect he would. Did you see his face turn twenty shades of red when Olivia told him?" I let out a low whistle as I admired the pair, but soon my attention shifted to another couple in the almost empty shop. Two young men, heads huddled over the table, with one reaching a hand to cover the other's. It was an intimate moment, and I felt like I was intruding, but I couldn't help but smile when Bradley returned the gesture, holding the hand of the pledge I'd seen him exchanging glances with after Trent's murder. So that solved the mystery of the trashed love letters.

"Here we go, ladies." Barry set two boxes of donuts on the tabletop, opening them with a flourish.

The sweet yeasty smell blasted me full force, and my stomach gurgled while I patiently waited for the others to choose.

Barry grinned. "Dig in. I hear it's been a busy night. Mind if I join?" He motioned to an empty chair beside Olivia.

"We wouldn't have it any other way," Olivia said, pushing the chair out as both Skylar and I gawked.

We gave each other a side glance before snatching the first donut in sight. Though my tummy growled, I set the creme-filled donut on my plate and wiped my sticky fingers, managing to leave bits of napkin on the tips.

Leaning onto the table for support, I drew in a deep breath. "I suppose it's time to piece everything together, yeah?"

"What gave it away?" Olivia asked.

The cool fall morning frosted the windows overlooking a nearly empty parking lot, soon to bustle with college students ready for a new day of classes.

"We heard everything from inside Warren's stuffy closet. Ashton made certain to keep our phones on." Skylar's mouth puckered. "Are you aware that Warren has multiple bottles of cologne? Better yet, are you aware of how potent the smells are in a confined space? It's lucky we didn't pass out."

"We caught almost everything," Olivia said, her expression soft and light for the first time in ages. "However, we would like you to start from the beginning."

"Fine, but it's the shortened version. We've still got an exam to study for."

Skylar gripped my wrist, her face pale. "Which one?"

Olivia scoffed. "You mean to say you haven't studied yet? I practically gave away all the questions in our last class. It's Biology 2, after all. How difficult could it be?"

"Can we postpone it? I'm sure Detective Shaw will provide a note," Skylar pleaded, her desperation adding a faint pink hue to her otherwise flawless complexion. "Right, Kaitlynn?" With a tight grip on her donut, she squeezed so hard that the red filling plopped onto her plate.

"The test's in two days." I offered her an encouraging squeeze of the hand. "We'll study together, and if we have to stay up for the next while getting you test ready, then so be it."

Olivia groaned. "Only after a nap. Now get started, chica," she scolded playfully with Barry looking on at her like she was some kind of wonderful.

"What tied it together was the tattoos. Scratch that, *one* tattoo in general. Remember the dragon, bear, and snake?"

Skylar grimaced around a mouth full of donut. "How could we forget? We spent eons looking over those photos. I swear there are at least a few hundred women on campus with those tattoos somewhere on their bodies, but what of it? Which tattoo linked it together? The dragon?"

Not much got past Skylar, and with her unusual gift, she would be unstoppable someday if only she'd honed it.

"Yes, the blue tailed dragon more specifically, which got me thinking about Professor Fletcher."

Skylar raised an eclair like a white flag, her speech muffled by another hefty bite. "Professor Fletcher, had a basic dragon. No blue tail."

"Exactly," I affirmed with a smile. "Her tattoo was different because of Connor."

I allowed a moment for my words to sink in, watching their puzzled expressions.

"And Trent's tattoo wasn't the dragon," I clarified, anticipating their realization.

They remained silent, as if waiting for a revelation.

"Trent didn't tattoo anyone," I said.

Skylar froze, her donut dropping to the plate with a thud. "Oh. My. God."

"What?" Olivia eagerly asked, searching both our faces while Barry, who hadn't been privilege to any of our information sat quietly.

Skylar's mouth opened and shut multiple times. "Um, okay." She dabbed a napkin at her lips. "Those tattoos were Connor's then."

"Yes and no," I said.

"You've lost me," Olivia said with a flick of her wrist. Her interest in the donuts revived, she chose a sprinkled concoction, ignoring the half-eaten one on her plate.

I waited on Skylar's dubious expression for a minute. It was like watching a clock's wheels turn, a precision I could only marvel at.

"So Connor tattooed all those women with a dragon because he was... *jealous?*" Skylar asked, locked on me this time with a kruller.

"I'm lost," Olivia interjected. To Barry, "Are you lost?"

He nodded, lovingly tucking a strand of hair behind her ear, only remotely interested in our conversation.

Sky stared at me, the spark of realization igniting in her eyes, before she slammed her fist on the table. "Connor tattooed each girl with a dragon because Fletcher had a dragon, is that right?" Sky exclaimed.

I grinned. "Exactly. Remember when we spoke with Professor Fletcher in her office? She admitted to a relationship with Trent, but she hadn't planned on him drugging her and taking lewd photographs as leverage. Trent never drugged her. It was Connor."

"How?" Olivia was fully engrossed, momentarily forgetting Barry as she leaned forward, donut in one hand.

"Connor supplied the water bottle," I explained. "He slipped in the drug and gave it to Trent."

Olivia's eyes nearly popped out of her head. "So Fletcher thought it was Trent, not Connor. That sneaky little jerk. But if Trent never drugged Fletcher, and you say he never tattooed anyone, then he *wasn't* part of the fraternity ring?"

I grinned. "There wasn't a ring. The other guys weren't part of it either. It was all a mirage. A facade. Ashton, Connor, and Warren were the only ones a part of this whole thing."

"Victoria," Skylar added.

We all pointedly stared at her.

She sipped on her coffee and met us with a dubious stare. "She's a part of the team too."

My heart skipped a beat. "I forgot about her."

"Really?" Skylar snorted. "She's sleeping with your boyfriend."

"Ex," I blurted.

"Ex-boyfriend. Killer extraordinaire." She laughed, which abruptly stopped at the sour looks. "Too soon?" She mouthed "okay" and stuck her mug up to her nose, covering her flushed face.

"Victoria wasn't a part of this whole thing, was she?" Olivia asked.

I thought hard over all the evidence and confessions we'd heard, and then shook my head. "No. She wasn't. At least, not about the whole Fletcher thing or tattooing. She *was* privy to Warren's sister, but Victoria believed Ashton. I'm sure of it."

"That Trent was responsible?" Skylar asked.

"Victoria believed it was Trent from the start. Ashton fooled a lot of people."

"So Connor was the attacker," Skylar summarized, . "Ashton was a perv, Warren joined the frat to watch over Connor, and Ashton concocted the whole tattoo ring to throw off the scent of his real goal, to crush Trent."

"Sort of," I replied. "It was only Ashton and Connor tattooing anyone."

"But there was a bear tattoo on one of those women, remember?" Olivia asked.

"Yes, but there was only one, and that's Warren's girlfriend. She calls him Bear."

"ALRIGHT," Skylar said, "but how did you piece it together with the dragon?"

"Ah," I breathed, "that was the tricky part. All those dragons, right? Then I remembered Professor Fletcher had a fetish for dragons. In her office, there were framed Japanese pictures of dragons all over her walls, but there was a particular one on her desk I saw, the only one that was framed. It had a blue tail, which Connor must have seen. So enamored with her, I bet he went to her office at least once. Anyway, when Fletcher bent over, I noticed a dragon on her and didn't give it much thought."

"So?" Oliva pressed.

"*So* it was different than all the others. Fletcher has a dragon with a gray tail."

Barry frowned. "Gray? Dragons don't have gray tails." His deep voice rang out in the small shop.

I flinched, forgetting he was even there. For a man of his size, he sure was quiet. "True, but I'm guessing Fletcher had it done that way on purpose."

"What for?" Olivia asked, her pretty features scrunched in earnest.

"Trent's eyes were gray."

Skylar gasped. The room got eerily quiet. Neither of us spoke until a crash in the kitchen snapped us out of it.

Barry hopped up. "Gotta run. Dad's a little clumsy in mornings, and the breakfast rush will be here shortly. No hurry, ladies," he added as we each grabbed our purses, ready to leave. None of us wanted anyone seeing us this haggard. "Stay as long as you want." To Olivia he said, "If you don't have anything to do tonight, would you like to take a walk by the lake? I can take you for dinner afterwards." His face shone down on Olivia's in hope.

Skylar and I zeroed in on Olivia's upturned face, waiting for the stuttering and flushed expression, but this time, Olivia sat up straight and beamed up at him. "I'd love that. Pick me up at seven?"

"Will do," Barry grinned. "Ladies, it's been a pleasure. Come back anytime. Oh, and call me next time you need backup." He patted his biceps. "These come in handy."

Off he went behind the counter, disappearing into the kitchen.

"He's good for you," I commented over a sip of coffee. I needed all the caffeine I could get for studying and classes without so much as a wink of sleep.

Olivia ran her index finger over the rim of her mug, lost in thought. "He is. Barry's a real gentleman, and after what we've experienced, I won't settle for anything else."

I reached over and squeezed her hand. "I should hope not. You deserve the world, Olivia, and Sky, you too." I patted Skylar on the back. "But ladies, we've got a day of studying ahead, and I'm in real need of a shower."

We packed up to leave, and when we set foot out into the cool fall morning, the sun peeked through the clouds, its orange rays breaking through the darkness that had not only enveloped the night but our hearts too. My thoughts were of Trent and how he'd sacrificed himself to protect all the other women on campus. I'd really mistaken him for a jerk, but he was only a protector.

We buckled up in the car, the heater roaring, and backed out.

"We'll attend his funeral," Skylar stated.

Goosebumps erupted all over my body. It was as if she'd read my thoughts. I don't think I'll ever get used to her abilities.

I let out a noisy sigh. "That would be lovely."

"Trent was a decent man, and he deserves a proper sendoff. Hey," Skylar's forehead scrunched up, "does Detective Shaw know all of this?"

"I told her as much during our short interrogation. She believes she's got enough evidence to put Connor and Ashton away for quite some time, thanks to you both."

Olivia grunted. "We didn't do anything."

"The recording, Liv," Skylar said from the back seat. She playfully nudged Olivia's shoulder.

"Oh right! " We never stopped recording. Brilliant, Kaitlynn. It's a relief to know those creeps are off the streets, hopefully for good."

"Just promise me something? Promise me that if we're ever in trouble, no matter how big or small, that we'll be open to each other? Reach out, okay?"

Olivia and Skylar nodded. "We promise," they both said.

"All right, ladies. Who's ready for a hot shower and a nap?"

I zoomed down the road toward my apartment, yet to shake the uneasiness of what had happened. Ashton had fooled a lot of people, me included, and it left a nasty taste in my mouth. I'd let my guard down to the point I missed all those signs, and as I pulled into my parking spot and turned off the engine, I promised myself that I'd never do that again.

As my friends skipped over to the stairwell leading up to my front door, I smiled. I couldn't have done any of this without their help, and I realized I'd fight to the death for each one if necessary.

"Are you coming?" Olivia's voice echoed from the doorway where she and Skylar stood linked arm in arm. Their faces were radiant and carefree, but as my gaze fixed on Olivia, a heaviness settled in my stomach. I recoiled at the intensity of it. Trembling, I focused on Olivia, who waved her hand enthusiastically, urging me to join them.

"What's holding you up?" she teased as she huddled closer to Skylar for warmth. "Hurry up, slowpoke!"

As quickly as the sensation jolted through me, it dissipated into the morning light, yet the unease lingered, settling in my heart. Shaking my head, I shook it off and stepped out of the car, attributing it to lack of sleep. As I approached Olivia and Skylar, Olivia reached out for me, and the instant our hands met, a surge of electricity shot through me.

"Ouch," Olivia giggled. "That was some static."

Skylar's smile faltered. "Are you okay?" she asked, extending a hand toward me.

I waved her off with a wink. "I'm fine. Let's go warm up."

I opened the door and they bounded up the stairs, but the disturbing image I had seen kept me rooted to the spot.

In that brief moment of static, I had glimpsed a horrifying scene: Olivia's lifeless body on the floor, her head battered.

"Hello!" Olivia shouted from the top of the stairs. "Are you coming or what?"

Her beautiful smile brought me back to reality. Last night's debacle all about did me in. So much so that I was starting to see things. I launched up the stairs, shutting the door behind me.

"Hey, guys? Another promise."

Once inside the apartment, they turned and shook out of their jackets, tossing them on my sofa.

"What's that?" Olivia asked, rubbing her hands together for warmth.

"Let's steer clear of murder mysteries for a while."

They both giggled. "Romantic comedies it is!" Skylar raised her arms high in the air, swaying to imaginary music as they headed for my bathroom closet.

"Yep," I murmured to myself. "Life is good."

Taking in the interior of my apartment, I noticed the worn couch and sofa, the childhood pictures on the wall, and the refrigerator, which I knew to be empty.

This was *living*.

No longer under my mother's roof, I wrapped my arms around myself and sighed, releasing all the tension that had built up over the past few days.

With a grin, I headed toward the giggles and squeals. With friends like this, nothing could ever bowl me over again. Yeah, life *was* good!

SUBSCRIBE FOR UPDATES and discounts at kduptonwrites.com. Click on the SUBSCRIBE tab at the top of the website and get reading!

Read *Graded for Murder* next!

GRADED FOR MURDER

Graded for Murder is next. Happy reading! kduptonwrites.com

ALSO BY K.D. UPTON

The Kaitlynn Dahl Mysteries

Graded for Murder

Snapshot to a Killer

Key to Murder

The Daisy Day Mysteries

Murder in the Orkneys

Mystery of the Charred Bones

Mystery of the Norse Runes (coming soon!)

The Skylar Night Ghost Mysteries

Ominous Visions, Grave Decisions

The Protectorate (Supernatural Suspense Action Adventure)

The Protectorate

The Guardians

Forefathers (coming soon!)

The Cosmo Pritchard Mysteries

Barn of Shadows (novella)

AVAILABLE ON KDUPTONWRITES.COM